DEMON

JOEL ABERNATHY

Copyright © 2023 by Joel Abernathy

All rights reserved.

No portion of this book may be reproduced in any form without written permission from the publisher or author, except as permitted by U.S. copyright law.

Falling in love with an obsessive serial killer was the last thing on my to-do list.

I was born into a world of villains, so it came as no great surprise when my brothers fell for the most twisted monsters of all. A sociopathic fixer. A psycho sadistic cop whose name belongs in the dictionary next to corruption.

Maybe I'm the one who's crazy, thinking I could have any semblance of a normal life. The worst part is, I can't even blame them for my not-so-perfect marriage crashing and burning, or my struggles as a single father. When my young son goes missing and a ransom note turns up demanding a trade for the serial killer my brothers-in-law keep locked in a basement, though?

Yeah, I'm blaming them for that. And I'll tear the world apart to get my kid back--even if it means keeping Demon leashed at my side.

James is something far more dangerous than Silas and Malcolm. He's an unhinged, self-righteous killer who's on a mission to punish the sinners who broke him in the first place.

He's also my only hope of ever seeing my son again. When you embark on a journey through hell, you want a demon on your team.

It's when he ends up in my bed that it's a whole different problem.

Author's Note: Demon is an intense, high-heat, high-angst MM Mafia Romance brimming with violence and mayhem. This book is significantly darker than the previous two. Please check the author's website for a full list of story elements that may be unsettling for some readers. While each book in the series features a different couple and is technically a standalone, it is recommended to read them in order.

1

LUCA

"You're late," Malcolm announced from the grill as soon as I walked off the back patio and into the back yard, where a barbecue was in full swing.

My younger brother, Valentine, gave him a scolding look. "Don't be rude," he said, pushing up from his wicker chair. He bounded over to me like the six-foot Labrador retriever he was and knelt down to grin at the kid at my side. "Hey, little man! You ready for some fireworks?"

"Yeah!" Timothy said brightly.

"Come on, let's go grab some sparklers," Val said, offering his hand.

"Nothing that could blow off any fingers," I called after them. "Or limbs!"

"It's good Val finally has someone his own mental age to play with," Enzo mused, offering me a beer.

I took it gratefully, popping the top off on the edge of the picnic table. We were all gathered at the family house, which Enzo and Silas were currently living in. It was the head of operations, and Enzo was the head of the Family, so it just made sense.

Even though I was pretty sure living in upper-class suburbia was Silas's own personal idea of hell, he didn't really seem to mind. He would do anything for my brother, and despite my initial—and current—trepidations about their relationship, even I could see that.

He definitely looked out of place, though, with his shock-white hair and five-piece gray suit that had probably cost the entire GDP of a small country.

"Sorry we're late. My lawyer needed to get my signature on some paperwork, and it took a lot longer than I thought," I said, running a hand through my hair. It was getting longer than I usually let it since I hadn't exactly had time to get a moment's sleep, let alone keep an appointment with my barber. If I didn't watch it, I was going to be a hippie like Val soon enough.

Meanwhile, he and Enzo both looked happier and healthier than they ever had. I was the middle brother, but I was starting to feel older than Enzo and I was sure I looked it lately. There were a few strands of gray in my dark hair now, and it was no mystery how they'd gotten there.

Enzo frowned, a tinge of concern in his eyes. "Don't worry about it. Everyone knows you're going through a lot right now. Is everything still on track with the divorce, or…?"

"Yeah," I answered. "Everything should be finalized next month."

"Wow," Enzo said, leaning back in his chair. "How are you feeling about that?"

I saw a flash of light out of the corner of my eye and looked up to see Valentine running like hell while Timothy chased him with a handful of sparklers, laughing maniacally.

"I'm not sure," I admitted, taking a gulp of beer. "I guess I haven't been letting myself think about it, you know? My marriage is over. Has been for a long time. Now, it's just about making it official and picking up the pieces." Even as I spoke, it sounded like my voice was coming from somewhere else.

"Still," Enzo said, clearing his throat. "I know talking about feelings and shit isn't really our thing, but if you ever need to talk…"

"I know," I said, taking another drink. "Thanks."

"All right, all the overly processed and wholly undesirable bits of the cows and pigs have been sufficiently cooked to avoid food poisoning and other liabilities," Silas announced, setting a plate of grilled hamburgers and hotdogs down on the table in front of us. "Time to celebrate a congressional document not a single goddamn person at this table has ever actually read."

"Festive," I said flatly, looking over at Enzo. "We gotta do Christmas at your place this year."

Enzo rolled his eyes, taking the plate from his husband. "He'll be on good behavior. No promises about Thanksgiving, though."

Valentine came over and sat Timothy in his booster seat before sitting down at the table. I knew trying to get him back was a lost cause, but the truth was, I really didn't mind having a babysitter at family events. It was the only time I got a break these days.

And that made me feel like even more of a shit parent. Was there a father's version of postpartum depression? Because if so, I was all but certain I had it.

Even when Timothy was over at Carol's, which seemed to be less and less often, it wasn't like I actually got a break. All I did was worry.

I worried that she wasn't paying enough attention to him, and that he was going to start picking up on the same apathy that had characterized our marriage for the last couple of years. I worried that she was going to dump him with her parents while she went out partying again with her friends, probably looking for the next guy she could bail on. I worried that she was going to do another one-eighty about being a parent, go for the full custody she'd initially shunned, and decide she was so pissed off at me that she wasn't going to let me see him at all.

Given my family's reputation, she would probably have a pretty easy time of it in the court system.

Even now, I found myself zoning out on the conversation because the war going on in my thoughts never ended. Malcolm and Silas were talking shop, and I usually zoned out as a matter of self-preservation, but lately, I was having a hard time keeping my eyes open for other reasons.

"Luca?" Valentine's voice cut through the noise, and I looked up. Judging from the fact that he and everyone else at the table were giving me worried looks, I had zoned out for a little longer than I thought.

"Yeah, sorry," I said, rubbing my eyes. "What is it?"

Valentine and Malcolm exchanged a look, and I could tell from the former's expression that he was saying with his eyes, "See? I told you so."

"Timmy was just asking if he could see the cat," Valentine said pointedly.

"The cat?" I asked, blinking. "What cat?"

Now Silas and Enzo were exchanging a look. They'd all been together a fraction of the time Carol and I had, and yet both couples acted like they'd formed a telepathic bond or something.

"Silas picked it up at a job," Enzo said unhappily. He always had been more of a dog person, but Silas was allergic. Allegedly. "Now we have a cat."

"*You* have a cat?" I asked doubtfully, looking over at my brother-in-law.

"Her name is Hannibal," Silas said proudly.

"Do I even want to know why her name is Hannibal?" I asked, very much against my better judgment.

"When I found her, she was eating a man's face," Silas said matter-of-factly.

I gagged on the bite of hotdog I had just taken. Really should have known better. "Wish I hadn't asked."

Valentine grimaced, but that didn't stop him from eating.

"She's a tortoiseshell," Silas continued. "Did you know some of them are chimeras? They absorb each other in the womb.

You can DNA test a leg, and it'll come back with completely different DNA from the head."

"I had a case like that a few years back," Malcolm mused. "Video surveillance had the guy walking into the murder scene, cut and dry, but we couldn't get a DNA match. Turned out he'd absorbed a twin in the womb. Should've seen how smooth his lady arms were."

"Huh," Enzo snorted. "Talk about skipping leg day."

"Okay, you know what? Fine, he can see your mutant cannibal cat," I said, holding up my hands. "Please, just stop discussing crime scenes in front of my kid."

"Come on, kiddo," Silas said, lifting Timothy out of his booster seat. "Let's go see Hannibal."

"Kitty!" Timothy cried happily.

Much to my chagrin, the kid loved Silas. Malcolm, too. Then again, in the world we inhabited, being surrounded by overprotective psychopaths probably wasn't the worst thing that could happen to him. At least they gave more of a damn about him than his own mother did.

"Don't worry," said Enzo. "The cat's had all its shots."

"That's really the least of my concerns right now," I muttered.

"You look rough," said Malcolm. "When was the last time you slept?"

"Fuck you, too, Mal."

"He's just worried about you, Luca," said Valentine. "We all are."

Chapter 1

Judging from the way Enzo had fallen silent, this wasn't the first time they had talked about this. Behind my back.

"What is this, an intervention?" I asked.

"If it needs to be," Malcolm said. I was starting to feel like I was on the other end of one of his interrogations.

I sighed. "I've been burning the candle at both ends lately, but I'm fine."

"You don't look fine," said Valentine. "You know, there's a reason sleep deprivation is used as torture. You have to get some rest. Why don't you let Mal and I take Timmy for a night or two? Give you a chance to catch up on some sleep."

I glanced between them warily. "Look, I appreciate the offer, but you guys have your own shit to take care of, and I really don't want my kid coming back talking like John Wayne."

"Someone's gonna have to teach the kid to shoot straight and it sure ain't gonna be you, pretty boy," Malcolm scoffed. "I've seen you at the range."

I glowered at him. "No one has to teach him any of that shit, actually. I don't want Timothy to have anything to do with this bullshit. Not our family business, and sure as hell not yours."

"That's not very practical, Luca," Enzo argued. "The kid is a DiFiore. He should know where he comes from."

"Knowing and being a part of it are two different things," I countered. "You want an heir, you and Silas can go have your spunk spun together in a turkey baster or whatever the fuck it is they do now, and leave me out of it."

Enzo just rolled his eyes.

"We should do that," Valentine said, clinging to Malcolm's arm as he leaned into his husband. "Imagine having a bunch of tiny little yous and mes running around."

"Thanks for giving him ideas, Luca," Malcolm said flatly.

"Please, let me watch Timmy for the weekend?" Valentine pleaded. "I'm practically a bored housewife these days, anyway. I take my patients out of my downstairs office, so I'll be able to keep an eye on him the whole time. And I promise, I'll make Mal lock everything up in the safe."

"Why do I get the feeling you're not just talking about the guns?" I asked warily.

Before Valentine could answer, the sliding glass door that led into the house opened and Timothy came running out, carrying a fat black-and-orange cat in his arms as he raced across the lawn like a clumsy fugitive with Silas close on his tail.

"Be careful," Silas called after the little guy, looking more distressed than I had ever seen him. "And don't stroke her fur backwards, she's very sensitive."

"My husband, the cat whisperer," Enzo said dryly.

I sighed, running a hand down my face. "I guess I could use a little sleep. But just for the night. And if anything goes wrong, I'll have my phone on the whole time."

"Of course," Valentine said eagerly.

"His bedtime is seven," I continued. "And don't let him watch anything that would've made you piss the bed when you were a kid. Especially if it has puppets. He hasn't been the same since he saw that H.R. Pufnstuf VHS tape up in the attic."

"Seven sharp, and no puppets," Valentine said patiently. "No big deal. Hey, Timmy! You want to come stay with me and Uncle Mal for the night?"

"Yeah!" Timothy cried, finally handing the cat back to a very harried-looking Silas.

The cat didn't seem bothered, but Silas held her close to his chest and stroked her fur tenderly like some kind of Bond villain. At least until he noticed Enzo was filming him and laughing his ass off.

My family was fucked up. Of that, there was no question, but as tempting as it had been to isolate myself after the divorce, it was good to be around them. And seeing my son so happy and surrounded by people who loved him was all I could really ask for.

Even if half of them were psychopaths.

2

JAMES

Footsteps echoed through the cement corridor outside, and I knew immediately from their particular cadence that it was Silas coming to pay me a visit.

Right on schedule.

I heard the automatic lock chirp outside before the door swung open, scraping along the floor, and in walked Silas, looking like a bored god among bacteria.

When it came to the company he usually kept, that wasn't too far off.

"Well, I'm impressed," he said in his usual silken voice, casually walking over to stand in front of the glass separating us. "That's the second guard this week you've pushed to a nervous breakdown."

"Please. That's old terminology," I scoffed. "Tyler had a *mild* psychotic break, but the last one was full psychosis. That's what you get for picking up the State Department's leftovers."

"What can I say? The NSA was running dry," he said flatly. "Out of curiosity, what exactly is it you're trying to accomplish?"

"Isn't it obvious?" I asked. "Your attention."

Silas's eyes narrowed. It was a slight shift, but I had always been able to read even the most minor physiological changes in anyone like a book, ever since I was a child.

And Silas? He was my favorite book. One I never grew tired of rereading.

That trait was the reason he'd once found me so useful, and now, I was going to make sure it was the thing that made me a thorn in his side.

"Congratulations, then. You've got it," he said, dragging a chair over from the corner of the room.

I winced. The sound of it scraping across the concrete was like rusty nails digging into my brain. This place was so far underground, it practically doubled as a sensory deprivation chamber.

He sat down, leaning over the back of the chair to watch me for a few moments, his silver eyes cold and appraising as they studied me.

I knew that look. It was one he'd given me a thousand times before. The look that made it clear I was the lab rat and he was the scientist. Right now, he was trying to figure out the most expedient way of taking me apart without rendering me useless.

It gave me that warm, tingly feeling all over. Just like old times.

"Come on, Silas," I sneered. "You can lie to everyone, even yourself, but you can't lie to me. He must bore you. Such a simple, guileless creature... Surely the novelty of living with your suburban pet mobster has worn off by now. You crave chaos. You need it, and I'm that, if nothing else."

"You are," he agreed. "And there was a time when that appealed to me, but I've outgrown chaos. As for me finding Enzo boring, you're the one who's lying to yourself if you really think that. But given the fact that you went to such lengths to try to take him from me, I don't think that's the case."

Rage washed through me at the sound of Enzo's name on his lips, but I knew better than to show it. For years, Silas had tried to purge me of all emotion and make me like him. He'd failed, but he had succeeded in teaching me to mask it. Especially from him.

To add insult to injury—or rather, murder, considering the fact that he had tried to kill me in a literal explosion—he had gone for someone who was my exact opposite in every regard. Enzo was the kind of man who spent hours in the gym and had probably never even owned a library card. He was broad and muscular, a big brute of a mafioso through and through. I was tall but lean, and now gaunt from months spent in isolation and near-starvation. I was still attractive—there was no point in the false humility of denying that—but there was something about my frigid blue eyes that seemed to put people off.

Chapter 2

It didn't matter, though. The one man I'd ever wanted was attracted to my particular brand of crazy—or at least, he had been.

Apparently, Silas now preferred big brown-eyed puppy dogs to a man who could kill without a second's remorse.

"It won't last," I said once I trusted myself to speak without showing weakness. "Eventually, you'll grow bored of sharing your bed with that buffoon. You'll long for the company of someone who's your intellectual equal."

"Is that what you are?" he asked, his tone as cutting as his words.

I scoffed a laugh. "That's why you're here, isn't it? I'm sure you've worked up some pretense. Something you want to question me about. Maybe even a bit of torture. And by all means, I'm more than happy to give you what you've been missing. I doubt that milquetoast boy can take even a fraction of your sadistic urges. It must be torture, having to be gentle. Pretending to be human."

"You'd be surprised what Enzo can take," he said dryly. "But there is something I'd like to know, actually."

"I'm all ears, love," I said, leaning back in my chair.

"Alec Loran," Silas said, staring me down. "Where is he?"

"Ahh," I purred. "Now there's a name I haven't heard in a long time. Is he still running papers?"

"I know you went to him to start over," said Silas. "That's the only way you could possibly have stayed off my radar for as long as you did."

"You're right," I mused. "I did. And I can see why you'd be seeking him out, considering you hired him to help make me disappear. It's disappointing when things don't go our way, isn't it?"

The flash of irritation in his eyes told me I was right. Of course I was. And Silas was getting weaker, because once upon a time, he wouldn't have betrayed anything at all.

No... not weaker. He was becoming human, and for a man like him, that was so much worse.

"Are you going to tell me, or not?" he asked boredly.

"I'll tell you," I said, leaning forward to look up at him through the veil of my overgrown hair. "If you fuck me."

His sharp features turned downward into a mask of callous disapproval. He stood up and turned around without a word, but when he reached the guard at the door, he paused. "Don't feed him for a few days," he said to the guard in a frigid tone I was well acquainted with. "And no water until he starts showing signs of severe dehydration."

"Yes, sir," the guard said, nodding in acknowledgment.

The door shut behind them, and I felt my shoulders trembling with barely contained laughter as I heard Silas walking away.

The metallic taste of blood in my mouth alerted me to the fact that I had bitten my lip.

Was I laughing, or crying? It was hard to tell, now that I was thinking about it.

I wasn't really sure there was that much of a difference when it came to him.

3

LUCA

I had pictured some hole in the wall or maybe a cave, but as I followed Silas through the winding corridors of the underground prison, I was quickly realizing this place was fully functional, including the guards stationed around every corner.

When Silas had called and asked me to take a watch for his secret prisoner, I had been surprised to say the least. Apparently, the guy who was originally supposed to be with him had gone MIA or something. I knew from Valentine's bitching that Silas and Malcolm had been alternating twelve-hour shifts to make sure they had coverage, so I'd agreed for my brothers' sakes.

That and there was a part of me that was admittedly curious, considering I was the one person who'd never met the infamous James, AKA Demon, AKA Valentine's former boss, Chris.

He was a man of many names and I couldn't help but be curious enough to want to put a face to them, even if it went against my usual policy of having as little to do with Silas's and Malcolm's bullshit as possible.

And that included the secret underground prison that was undoubtedly violating a metric ass-ton of international and domestic laws.

"I have had reason to use it over the years," my brother-in-law remarked, as if reading my thoughts.

"I'm sure you have," I muttered. "How many prisoners are here at the moment?"

"At the moment, just James and a former associate who betrayed me," he answered nonchalantly. Like keeping people in his own personal dungeon was just par for the course.

For him, it probably was.

It wasn't like I had any sympathy for Demon. Far from it. But it was still a lot to get used to. I thought the world I had grown up in was harsh and ruthless, but we had rules, at least. For the most part, people abided by them.

This world had rules, too. People like Silas and Malcolm simply made them and followed them only if and when they saw fit.

"You disapprove?" Silas asked in a knowing tone.

"Not at all. I mean, who among us *doesn't* have a privately funded dungeon to keep his enemies without due process or rule of law?"

Silas stopped walking, and when he turned around, I was surprised to find that his expression was one of amusement rather than the annoyance I had expected. "If you'll remember, turning him over to the police was originally the plan. Until he targeted your brothers."

"Doesn't change the fact that you had this place ready," I countered.

Silas paused as if to consider it. "No. It doesn't."

He kept walking before stopping in front of a large door at the end of the hallway.

"You should be aware of something," he said. "James is remarkably adept at manipulation. He knows no boundaries and no limitations."

"What are you saying? You think I'm going to have a meltdown or something?" I asked, not bothering to hide my irritation.

"Stronger men have," he remarked, like the complete jerk he was.

I frowned. "Screw you, too."

"It's nothing personal," he said with a shrug. "It would be unkind not to warn you of what you're in for. You should treat his threats as actionable out of an abundance of caution, even if he is trapped in here."

"Seriously?" I asked. "We're what, how many stories underground?"

"A caged animal is always the most dangerous," Silas said calmly. "But it's not just the physical threats. He knows how to get inside your head. He'll make you question things. He'll make you angry. He'll isolate your weakness and prey on it in ways you never thought were possible. He elevates mindfuckery to an art form."

"Yeah, I can see why you two were so close," I said dryly. "Real shame it didn't work out."

"You should resist the urge to engage with him, no matter what he says," said Silas. "No matter how he tries to agitate you. You give him anything and he *will* find a way to use it against you."

"Yeah, I got it," I muttered. "Trust me, I have no intention of striking up a conversation with this creep."

Silas stared at me for a few moments with that blank expression, like he was running some kind of retinal scan on me, before he finally turned around and swiped his card in the reader on the wall.

The two silver doors slid open with a rush of air. I had pictured some dank cell with iron bars, but this place looked more like a supervillain's holding chambers. The light gray walls probably made the space look larger than it was, but it was still unnecessarily huge for one person.

Not that the prisoner had all of it to roam. There was a smaller glass box in the interior of the room, ten by ten at the most, furnished solely with a bare mattress on the floor, a toilet in the corner, and a metal chair presently occupied by the room's lone occupant.

I stopped on the other side of the door and let Silas be the first to walk closer as I studied the cell. It was the first time I had ever come face-to-face with the infamous Demon, and I wasn't sure what I was expecting, but it certainly wasn't the man in front of me.

He wasn't particularly tall or muscular. In fact, he looked borderline emaciated with gaunt cheekbones and a less

Chapter 3

than imposing build, although that might easily have been a result of the year and change he'd spent in captivity. He certainly wasn't getting the ritzy treatment. His sun-starved skin was unnaturally pale, with dark circles rimming eyes the iciest shade of blue I'd ever seen. They made Silas's look almost warm in comparison. His light brown hair was shaggy, framing a hard jaw and angular features that might have looked pleasant enough if it weren't for those eyes.

The way they followed Silas as he walked into the room was nothing shy of menacing. Like a predator stalking his prey —and I was pretty sure it was a rare occurrence anyone saw my brother-in-law as that.

He didn't pay me any attention, which was just as well. As unassuming as he had looked at first glance, there was something about the guy's energy that had me on edge. Like two dissonant chords putting off an unnatural frequency the human ear just wasn't meant to hear.

"Look who it is," Demon said in a mocking tone. There was nonetheless something pleasant about it. Deep but not too deep. A bit on the husky side. His gaze traveled over to me, and the smile that tugged at his chapped lips immediately disabused me of any notion of pleasantry. "And you brought the boring brother. How fun."

I raised an eyebrow, but said nothing. If that was the worst he had, I wasn't really worried. Boring wasn't exactly an insult coming from a guy like him. Hell, boring was my five-year plan now that things were finally quieting down after the divorce.

"Consider yourself lucky I didn't bring Malcolm," said Silas.

Demon blew a puff of air through his nostrils. "You must have run out of guards you trust."

For a split second, irritation showed on Silas's usually blank face. Well, if nothing else, this creep was certainly capable of getting under Silas's skin. "I wonder why that might be."

Demon just grinned malevolently, leaning back in his chair. "You can't blame it all on me. I know how many resources you must be diverting to keep an eye on Enzo and the family business. That's the price of keeping a pet mafioso, I suppose. At least Malcolm picked an insignificant little nobody the first time around. Although, that didn't really work out so well for him, either, did it?"

Silas clenched his jaw and his gaze darkened. They were subtle shifts anyone else might not have noticed, but I was starting to think he was the one who needed to get a handle on *his* reactions.

"It's a temporary solution, I can assure you," said Silas. "Don't worry. I expect to hear that you've behaved yourself tonight—otherwise, your situation is going to be getting much worse."

"You promise?" James asked bitterly.

A dangerous, familiar smirk tugged at the corner of Silas's lips. "Don't tempt me." Silas turned back to me, but I could tell he was still annoyed. "Are you all right for me to take my leave?"

"Probably for the best," I answered, earning a glare from him.

"You have my number. I suggest you use it, even at the most minor provocation."

"Yeah, I got it." I sighed. "Get out of here. I'll be fine."

Silas took one more look at his prisoner and reluctantly nodded, unlocking the door to leave.

"Brave boy," Demon taunted, watching me from across the room like a cat watching a mouse.

I looked around the room for a chair and found one propped against the furthest wall. I got the feeling the other guards didn't like being any closer to their charge than they absolutely had to be.

Demon seemed somewhat surprised when I sank into the chair a few yards away from the glass. I didn't see any reason to be a fool, but I wasn't going to act scared of him, either. Even if I probably should have been.

"You got any telekinetic powers I don't know about?" I asked wryly.

"He really must be desperate if he sent the soft one."

"The soft one?" I echoed, raising an eyebrow. "And here I thought that was Val."

"He's the neurotic one," he clarified, as if it should be obvious. "Enzo's the dumb one, and you're the tender little darling who married his high school sweetheart. I thought that was obvious enough."

I scoffed. "Yeah, well, the marriage thing didn't work out too well, if that counts for anything."

The way his lips quivered at the corners was proof of what I already assumed, which was that he already knew. Of course he did. I wasn't sure how, but if Silas was right about him being a master manipulator, and he was even a fraction as good at it as Silas himself was, I figured he probably had ways of getting information out of people. It was admittedly a test to see just how much he knew—how much he cared to know—about me.

The results were disconcerting.

"Oh, yes," he remarked. "My sincerest condolences. I suppose that's the toll the family business takes, isn't it?"

"Something like that," I answered.

He smirked, leaning forward. "I guess you could look at the bright side."

"Yeah? And what might that be?" I asked, doing my best to sound bored. I knew Silas didn't want me talking to him at all, and there were probably plenty of reasons for that. Still, it seemed like more of a risk to appear weak, and there was no doubt in my mind that Demon would know my reasons for going radio silent. He would see Carol was a weakness he could exploit, and while there was probably some truth to that, too, I didn't need to confirm it for him.

"Things won't end the way they did between your parents," he replied innocently, even though I could tell he was watching closely for my reaction.

I gave a small laugh. "Never had all that much in common with my old man," I replied. "I don't think that's something I really needed to worry about."

"That's what they all say," he replied. "I'm sure that's what you told yourself when you held that darling baby boy in your arms for the first time, too. That you weren't going to be like your father. That you weren't going to fuck this one up the way he fucked up the three of you."

"Is there something wrong with that?" I asked. "With wanting to do better for your own child than your parents did for you?"

His lips quivered in a small smile. "The best laid plans of mice and men often go awry."

"Burns," I murmured, propping my left foot over my other knee. "Wouldn't have pegged you for the poetry type."

"Oh, I imagine there are all sorts of things you don't know about me," he remarked. "But I can't really say it goes the other way."

"No?" I asked. "You know a lot about me, do you?"

Demon paused as if to consider it. "I know you're probably the most level headed out of your family," he answered. "Level headed enough to know that this is all going to end disastrously. Disastrously enough to make *your* marriage look like a success story."

"You mean Silas and Malcolm," I said.

"Who else?" he asked. "If you let the foxes into the chicken coop, you can't be surprised when there's a bloodbath."

"I'm not sure how much allowing there was," I admitted, deciding not to deny it. "But it doesn't really matter what I think, does it? My brothers are both adults, and they can make their own decisions."

I could deny it for the sake of keeping up the appearance of a united front, but he was too smart to believe that. I was pretty sure my body language around Silas alone had told him all he needed to know about our relationship. And I really wasn't confident enough in my own abilities of deception to risk it. Especially not when doing so would only serve to convince Demon that he was poking at a weak point.

"Can they, though?" he challenged. "When you're dealing with monsters like Silas and Malcolm, can there ever really be such a thing as free will?"

"That's an interesting question," I remarked. "If I were in Philosophy 101, I'm sure it would give me plenty to think about."

His face split into a wide grin. "Bravo, Luca," he said in a tone of false praise. "Silas trained you well. Show no weakness."

"There's not much point in that, is there?" I asked. "We all have a weakness. Even you."

His amusement vanished so suddenly, I wondered if it was all a lark. Probably safer to assume that when it came to him. "*My* weakness isn't a precocious little simpleton helplessly toddling about."

For the first time, it was a struggle to mask my anger. "No, but I'm not so sure a six-foot-tall sociopath who only wants me alive so he can make me suffer would be a much better weakness to have."

James gave a dry, bitter laugh. "Yes, that certainly is what Silas would like the world to think. Maybe he even believes it."

"But you don't?" I asked. "If you actually think Silas still cares for you, maybe you're the dumb one."

It was a mistake to antagonize him. I knew that, but it wasn't like he hadn't already threatened me and mine before we

Chapter 3

had ever even met. I was pretty sure there was no way off his shit list once you were on it, so I might as well not appear intimidated.

Instead of retaliating, though, he laughed. "Wonderful. You're much more fun than the others. And there's more bite to you than I anticipated! What a pleasant surprise."

"Glad I could provide you some amusement," I said, looking pointedly around the empty space. "I imagine it gets a bit droll, day in and day out with nothing to do and no one to talk to other than people who wish you were dead."

"Oh, I wouldn't say that," he mused, leaning back in his chair to tap his temple. "Plenty to do in here."

"Right. You're some kind of super genius, huh?" I asked, folding my arms. "I guess you're plotting your great escape and revenge in there?"

"Something like that," he answered. "Would you like to know what I'm going to do to you when I get out?"

I pretended to consider it. "Can't say I do," I finally answered. "Never been a fan of spoilers. Surprises are nice from time to time."

He smirked. "We'll see how nice it ends up being. And we'll see if you're quite as brave when we're face-to-face."

"Bravery's not my thing," I said with a shrug. "Cowards live."

He chuckled. "Sometimes, yes. But they also die a thousand deaths."

"I've never bought into that," I admitted. "Just seemed like the kind of logic reckless sons of bitches like Enzo used to justify their actions."

"An interesting theory," he mused. "We could always put it to the test."

"If it makes you feel better to fantasize about what you're going to do to me when you get out of here, be my guest," I said with a shrug. "But there's two feet of bulletproof glass between us and a whole bunker on top, so I don't think you're going to be bringing those plans to fruition anytime soon."

"Maybe not," he conceded. "But it never hurts to plan ahead."

"And what exactly are you going to do when you succeed?" I asked. "Once you've got everyone who could interfere with your plans out of the way, what then? Are you just going to keep Silas locked up in a closet until he sees the error of his ways and falls madly in love with you?"

I could tell I had struck a nerve from the look in his eyes.

"Sorry, was that subject off-limits?" I asked. When he didn't answer, I pressed, "This is purely a matter of curiosity. Feel free to ignore the question, but what exactly do you see in him, anyway?"

"Are you asking because you want to know what *I* see in him, or what Enzo does?" he challenged. "Because I can guarantee you those are two very different answers."

I snorted. "Both, I guess."

He seemed to actually be giving it some thought. "They say familiarity breeds contempt," he finally replied. "I guess when all you have is contempt to start with, it yields different results."

"Is that it?" I asked doubtfully. "And here I thought it had something to do with the fact that he spared your life when he was hired to kill you."

Judging from the murderous glint in his eye, I had touched another nerve. I wasn't sure why I was even bothering with such a reckless game. It certainly wasn't in my character, and I usually didn't let people get to me. So far, he really hadn't, at least not as far as I was aware of.

No, this was something else. Strangely, I got the feeling it was... curiosity.

Maybe I was the dumb one.

Either way, Demon clammed up and didn't say a word for the rest of the night. Not that I really complained. I decided to leave well enough alone and pulled up the book I was reading on my phone. I had finished it and started another by the time Silas's new guard came to relieve me.

Considering the fact that Demon had yet to speak again, I was surprised when he called to me on my way out the door.

"Tell Silas to send you again sometime," he remarked. "It's been a pleasure."

I glanced back over my shoulder against my better judgment. "Sure," I said dryly. "Guess we'll see."

4

JAMES

Luca never came back after the first time. It was a disappointment, really. He was by far the least noxious of the three DiFiore brothers, and he wasn't too hard on the eyes, either. I was starting to get the appeal of big brown puppy eyes and more muscle than brains.

Instead, there were three new guards, two the usual type of hardened ex-special forces men I had expected. The third had the smooth demeanor of a typical mafioso, but with none of the social graces. The moment he walked in and I saw the glint of wickedness in his eyes, I knew he was trouble.

And I knew he was the form Silas's latest punishment had taken.

I'd tested it out by mouthing off once, and the first time, he'd dislocated my jaw. After that, he just seemed to be extra nasty for sport.

Chapter 4

That afternoon, it was apparently the world championship. I wasn't even sure what I'd said to piss this one off, but that was probably a result of the head trauma. As a giant fist came sailing toward my head, I just hoped it was something good.

As my head hit the stone floor with a nauseating crack, I felt the darkness ebbing in around the edges. I could see boots walking toward me. Each time they lifted off the floor, tacky strings of blood clung to them.

A familiar sense of déjà vu washed over me as I found myself transported out of the present moment and a memory from the past. The smell of blood and filth was the only connecting thread between them.

That and the darkness.

A sliver of light through the cracked door, eclipsed by the shadow of a man staggering across the room, bumping into furniture as he clutched his right eye. Blood was spilling through his fingertips as freely as the slurred curses pouring from his lips as he clawed at his wound.

I sat huddled in the armoire, my knees drawn to my chest, as I clutched the bloody kitchen knife in my palm. My body was trembling from adrenaline, my heart hammering like a rabbit's in my ears, so loud I could hardly hear the sounds of the furious man cursing out my mother as he staggered into the hallway.

I heard her voice, soft and cloying, as she tried to convince him to stay and let her treat him. It was the voice she always used on the men who came in and out of our small two-bedroom apartment like a revolving door.

With me, she had another voice. One that was harsh and serrated, just like the blade clutched in my small fist. I wasn't sure which version of her was real. I wasn't sure there was a real her.

Most of the time, I felt more like a doll than a real boy anyway, so maybe she was the same way. Maybe we weren't people at all. Maybe the men who came and used us both like toys until they got bored and left were right all along.

The front door slammed and shook the small trailer, and I hugged myself tighter, burying my face in my knees. I couldn't stop shaking, even though the edge of the knife was digging into my leg.

Light enveloped the small space, and when I looked up, all I saw was a familiar silhouette as my mother grabbed me by the wrist and dragged me out of the closet.

"James, what did you do?" she screamed, wrenching the blade from my grasp hard enough that the force sent me back onto the floor.

All I could do was stare up at her, my throat too tight to speak. I could still feel the man's hand wrapped around it. I'd been scared it would leave a bruise, and I would get in trouble if the teacher sent someone to our house again, so I'd used the knife I'd stolen out of the kitchen drawer the night before while my mother was in the other room with another man.

I wasn't even sure why I'd thought to take it, but I had stashed it beneath my mattress. It had been so easy. So much easier than the alternative, but now, as I found myself staring up at my mother, I realized I had avoided one punishment only to be faced with another.

She had beaten me to within an inch of my life that night, but it was worth it because none of the men who visited after that ever came to my room. And it had taught me a very important lesson.

The only person who was ever going to protect me was myself.

5

LUCA

Things were finally starting to get back to normal.

I had taken Valentine up on his offer to babysit a couple more times, and I had gotten caught up on sleep. At least as much as I was capable of catching up on in a few weeks' time after going on years of exhaustion, but still. I was starting to feel human again.

It was Carol's weekend to take Timmy, but when I went to her place to drop him off, she was gone. She wasn't answering her phone, so I figured she was either still out late at nine in the morning, or she had gotten drunk and slept through her alarm.

Either way, I wasn't about to leave him at her place, so I brought him back home. I figured she would call eventually, with some half-assed excuse and we could hash it out then, but when I saw her mother's phone number on my caller ID, I got worried.

"Heather?" I asked. "Is everything all right?"

Chapter 5

"Everything is fine, Luca," she said, her voice polite but strained. "I'm actually calling on Carol's behalf. She's... feeling a bit under the weather."

"I'm sorry to hear that," I said, glancing over at the corner of my office, where Timmy was playing with his toy train set. It was loud as hell, but it was the only way I got any work done during the day while he was awake.

We both knew Carol was hungover, so there was no real point in calling her out on the euphemism. Heather and Ken had always been kind to me, and they were family-oriented people. The fact that their daughter wanted nothing to do with her own kid got to them, and there was no point in making things more awkward than they already were.

"I hope she's feeling better," I replied.

"I'm sure she'll be fine." Heather sighed. "Since it's her weekend, we were really hoping to get to see Timmy. How would you feel about him just coming over to stay at our place? That kids' band he's so crazy about is doing a show in Braintree this afternoon, and we were going to take him. Besides, I'm sure you could use a break."

I hesitated. Something told me Carol had planned on dropping our son off at her parents anyway if they already had plans to take a daytrip on one out of the two days he was supposed to be with her.

It was fucked up, but a part of me was relieved. At least I knew he'd be around people who wanted to spend time with him. Ken and Heather were good grandparents, and considering the fact that Timmy didn't have any grandparents on my side, I wanted him to get to spend as much time with them as possible.

"Yeah, sure. I bet he'd love that," I said. "I am kind of behind on work, but I don't want to put you guys out."

"Nonsense. Now that Ken's retired and I'm only at the hospital part-time, we've got plenty of time on our hands. He'll be the highlight of our week," she said brightly, chuckling.

"Well, if you're sure, that would be great," I said. "But there's just one thing. Carol was going to keep him tomorrow night, too, and drop him off at preschool since I've got an appointment Monday morning."

"Oh, don't worry about that, we'll make sure he gets there on time," she assured me. "Just let us know and we can pick him up, too, if you need some more help."

"That's all right. I'll get his things ready and come drop him off at your place," I told her. After thanking her, I hung up and walked over to sit down next to Timothy, smiling. "Hey, kiddo. Any more room aboard the train?"

"No," he said, looking up at me with a grave expression. "Only dinosaurs."

I glanced over at the T-rex sticking out of the caboose and laughed. "I see. Silly me. How would you feel about spending the weekend at Grandma and Grandpa's and going to see Paw Parade?"

"Paw Parade?" His eyes widened and a huge grin spread across his face, beaming at a thousand watts. "Yeah!"

Chapter 5

I chuckled, ruffling the boy's hair. "Okay, then. Let's go brush your teeth and get your backpack."

To my relief, he didn't seem phased by the fact that he wasn't going to be seeing his mother, but I knew better than to think it would be so easy to patch things up forever.

Eventually, he was going to realize something was missing and want more than I could give him on my own. I just hoped that day wouldn't come anytime soon.

We spent the entire car ride to his grandparents' house singing along to his favorite song to the point where I was starting to question my sanity. Such was the life of a single father.

I was starting to feel like I might actually be getting the hang of it, but I didn't know if that was just the high I was still riding from getting seven whole hours of sleep in one night.

I felt guilty for feeling as relieved as I was when I finally dropped him off with Heather and Ken. It wasn't that I didn't love spending time with my kid. Timmy was my entire world, and he was the one thing I didn't regret about how my marriage had turned out. I would've done it all over again, knowing he was waiting on the other side, but I was just so fucking tired. Even when I wasn't.

It wasn't like it was always going to be this way, though. He wasn't going to be young forever, which made me feel even guiltier for the fact that I was wasting my limited time with him feeling this way. He deserved so much better than a dad who was always overwhelmed and a mom who didn't care where he was. I had to care enough for the both of us, all the while knowing deep down it still wasn't enough.

Catching up on work over the weekend took a good majority of my energy, and worrying about Timothy—even though I knew he was safe—took up the rest of it. Every time I started to relax, I felt guilty for enjoying the peace and quiet.

I wound up calling to check on him so many times I was surprised Heather hadn't blocked my number, but eventually, I had to just tell myself to chill the fuck out.

God, I was becoming neurotic.

Maybe I always had been, and parenting had just brought it out in me. Whatever the case was, I finally went to bed Sunday night before midnight for the first time in years. I proceeded to sleep right through my alarm.

And my meeting.

Fuck.

By the time I woke up with a mouth that felt like cotton, I realized it was well after two in the afternoon. And not only did I have half a dozen missed calls from Enzo and Johnny asking me why I hadn't showed up to my meeting, because I'd somehow managed to put my phone on silent while I was asleep, but I also had thirty minutes to get over to the preschool and pick Timmy up.

Shit.

Maybe I wasn't quite as caught up on all that sleep debt as I'd thought.

I took a shower at lightning speed and got dressed, somehow simultaneously sending what felt like my hundredth apology text to Enzo that week. I had always

Chapter 5

been someone he and the others could rely on, at the very least. I'd always taken pride in that, but now...

Fuck, I really had to get it together. When Johnny was the one constantly having to pick up the slack for me, there was a serious problem.

When I went to the school, I got the usual side-eye from a few of the other teachers and parents who were lingering in the hallway. I was late, and not for the first time. Being pulled in a million different directions was compounded by the fact that I never seemed capable of getting to one of them on time. Not that I was clueless enough to think my tardiness was the reason for all the suspicion.

The other parents knew who I was, and what my family did. And how could they not? Between Enzo's arrest for the murder of my best friend's father, our dad's death, and the shooting at Valentine's hospital, the DiFiore family had made its share of headlines over the last few years—and that was to say nothing of the usual criminal enterprises that had been our family's business for generations.

Right now, Timothy was still in preschool. He was too young for it to matter, but when he got older and his classmates were able to put two and two together, things would be different.

They certainly had been for me growing up. I didn't want that for him. I wanted him to have a normal life, or at least as normal as he was capable of having.

Sometimes I thought about leaving the capital-F Family altogether and moving somewhere we could start over, but then we'd both be separated from the only people we could actually count on. And then there was the fact that he'd be far from Carol if she ever got her shit together and decided to at least try being a decent parent.

Not that I was doing too hot myself at the moment.

I shook myself out of my thoughts as I approached the receptionist at the front desk. "Hi. I'm here to pick up Timothy."

She looked up from her phone, frowning. "Timothy DiFiore?"

"That's my son, yes," I said, trying to sound like someone who hadn't run out of patience three years ago.

She just blinked at me. "I'm sorry, but... he's not here."

"What do you mean, he's not here?" I demanded.

The girl behind the desk stared up at me with wide, fearful eyes, and I wasn't sure if it was my family reputation preceding me, or if I looked half as crazy as I felt right now, but either way, I didn't care.

"I... he was picked up already," she stammered, fumbling for a folder in the drawer under her desk. "There's a special pick-up, drop-off pass in his file for today. It says a family member checked him out. They had the passcode and everything."

"That was for drop-off only," I said gruffly. "His grandparents dropped him off. *I* was supposed to pick him up."

"Well, maybe they got confused?" she offered.

I frowned, taking out my phone. She was probably right, and I was freaking out for nothing, but it wasn't like Heather to make a mistake like that.

Of course, I was the one who was sleep deprived, so it was entirely possible I was the one who'd fucked up. I replayed our last conversation in my mind, trying to figure out if I'd said anything that would lead her to believe she was picking Timothy up after school, too. Or maybe Ken had misunderstood her relayed instructions and picked him up instead.

There were a thousand possible explanations, and I tried not to torture myself with the ugly ones as I waited for the phone to ring.

"Luca," Heather answered in a pleasant tone. "How's the little man? I hope he had a good time telling all his friends at school about the concert."

"He's not with you?" My voice sounded strained, but it didn't quite reflect the state of chaos swirling around inside my body.

There was a pause on the other end of the line that seemed to last forever, even though it couldn't have been for more than a second or two. "Wh-what? No. You said we only needed to drop him off this morning."

My heart was hammering again. I could hardly hear my own thoughts. "I'm at the preschool right now. He's not here. Could Ken have picked him up?"

"I—no, I don't think so," she answered, clearly flustered. "He was with me when I dropped him off this morning. He knew you were picking him up. We both said goodbye and everything."

"Can you ask him?" I asked, feeling like I was made up of a thousand threads all floating away from each other. "And Carol? Please."

"Of course," she said shakily. "I'll call them both right now on the landline."

The next few minutes were a blur, but while it was a struggle for me to get ahold of Carol at all, she answered on only the second ring for her mother. And I could tell from the panicked shrieks of indignation on the other line that she genuinely didn't have a damn idea where he was.

Which made the alternative so much fucking worse.

My first inclination was to call the police, but then I remembered I had a direct line to law enforcement. Even if Malcolm was technically "retired," he was still pulling more strings in the city in his unofficial capacity than he had throughout his long and infamous career as the chief of police.

Within twenty minutes, the school was crawling with cop cars, and Malcolm himself was interrogating the very unsettled desk worker who'd apparently let my kid go off with a complete fucking stranger.

She couldn't even remember what the prick looked like, except that he was wearing a suit, and looked "kind of like me," which was every fucking mobster with an undercut.

The security footage had to have something, I told myself. But when I saw the look on Malcolm's face, I knew better.

"What is it?" I demanded, stalking down the hall outside the police station offices. Technically, he shouldn't even have had free run of the place, but he had violated all the rules while he worked here, and no one ever stopped him from doing anything at all.

He just shook his head. "Someone took out the camera in the parking lot and in the school lobby half an hour before the desk worker says they checked him out. Whoever did this, it's a pro."

My stomach was already twisted into knots, but I felt like I was going to be sick despite not having eaten anything in the better part of twenty-four hours. "She's a new employee," I said, suddenly grasping at straws. "I only started seeing her a few weeks ago. She could be a plant."

"I already looked into the girl's background. She was a fucking candy striper," Malcolm muttered. "Besides, the other teachers corroborated her story and the other two who saw this guy checking Timothy out said the same thing. He had the passcode and the app, and he said he was Enzo. Whoever this is not only knew he was on the list of approved pick-ups, but knew you wouldn't be dropping him off today, so it was the perfect chance. Which means they've been watching you for a long damn time."

"This is bullshit," I seethed. "Who—"

I froze as my phone buzzed in my pocket. I snatched it out and looked at the screen only to see a text message that made my heart bottom out of my chest.

<Luca DiFiore, I believe we share a mutual acquaintance who is currently in your brother-in-law's possession. If you'd like to see your son again, you'll hand this acquaintance over to me, but all in good time. Await further instruction.>

"What was that?" Malcolm asked, frowning.

I handed the phone over, still completely numb. His eyes scanned the message quickly before his jaw clenched. "Fuck."

"It's him," I said through my teeth. "Silas said that freak you guys are keeping locked up had connections on the outside, and now they're trying to get him out, using my kid as bait!"

"We don't know that," Malcolm muttered, looking around. "Keep your voice down."

"Keep my voice down?" I shoved into his chest, snapping. "This is about my son! He's gone and it's your fucking fault!"

"Have you lost your goddamn mind?" Malcolm snarled, grabbing my arm and wrenching it behind my back before forcing me down a quieter hallway and away from the people giving us looks from further down the corridor. "You think committing assault in the middle of a fucking police station is going to help matters right now?"

He had a point, but I was too angry to listen. "You're the one who does whatever the fuck he wants. You're telling me you give a shit about law and order now?"

"Calm the fuck down, Luca," he growled, his grip loosening slightly on me. I expected he was going to hit me and I hoped he would. I had enough energy and aggression flowing through me that it needed an outlet. Instead, he put his hands on my shoulders and gave me an infuriatingly calm look as he said, "I know you're scared right now, but we're going to get Timmy back. Trust me. We will. We just have to do it the smart way. Thanks to that text, now we have a pretty fucking good idea of where to start."

Chapter 5

I felt my rage gradually beginning to subside, if only because of the promise of getting to take it out on a more appropriate target. "Yeah," I said through my teeth. "I guess we do."

6

JAMES

I wasn't sure if I had fallen asleep or passed out, but either way, when I heard footsteps coming down the corridor, my internal clock told me it was time for my favorite sadistic guard to come and play.

I'd already formulated a plan to bite off his fingers the next time they came anywhere near my face. Silas would undoubtedly make me pay for it, but for those few joyous moments I would get to spend watching the guard bleed and writhe around on the floor like a worm on a hook, it was a price I was more than willing to pay.

When the door opened and Silas walked in alongside Malcolm and Luca instead, I lifted my head, curious.

"Now this is a surprise," I said, smirking. The cut on my lip stung as it stretched and I tasted the metallic tinge of blood on my tongue. "Fancy a foursome, gentlemen?"

"Something like that," Malcolm said, stalking into the room. He stopped at the tempered glass, examining it like he was considering whether he wanted to try

Chapter 6

opening it with his fists. He looked down at me, his eyes brimming with disgust and rage that hadn't seemed to wane at all since the last time I'd seen him. He turned to Silas. "What the fuck happened to him? How am I supposed to torture the fucker if he's already on the brink of death?"

Silas frowned, his eyes narrowing as he studied me. "He must have pissed off one of the new guards."

I scoffed a laugh that ached deep in my chest. Probably the broken ribs. I was pretty sure he'd cracked my sternum on the last go, too. "Pretending like that wasn't part of your punishment?" I asked. "Who are you trying to impress?"

Silas frowned at me as if he didn't have a damn clue what I was talking about.

Not likely.

"Just open the fucking door," Luca said through his teeth. Out of the three of them, he was the one who looked like he wanted to tear me apart, limb by limb.

Interesting.

And here I thought I'd been downright hospitable during his first and last visit.

"I thought I'd scared you off," I mused.

Luca lunged, but Malcolm blocked him.

"Just settle down," Malcolm said. "We'll take care of it."

"Bullshit," Luca seethed, shoving him back. "He's part of this. I know he is, and it's your fucking fault!"

"I told you we shouldn't have brought him down here," Malcolm growled, ignoring Luca as he looked right at Silas. "He's too involved."

Before Silas could say anything, Luca snatched something out of his hand. The key card. I could tell the sudden bold move from the usually mild-mannered man had caught him off guard enough that he didn't react right away—at least until Luca had swiped the card across the reader on the surface of the glass, and the door clicked open.

Luca was barely inside when I saw a fist flying at me, and it connected with my face, sending me sprawling back, chair and all, to the other end of the cell. Luca was on top of me in an instant, straddling my chest and gripping my shirt in one hand with his right reared back in a fist, ready to punch me again.

"Where is he?" he seethed. "I know you had something to do with it, and I swear, if a hair on that kid's head is harmed, you'll fucking wish Silas had killed you."

I stared up into his eyes. His pupils were pinpricks and the whites reddened with exhaustion and rage. The eyes of a madman. Or a terrified man. In his case, whatever circumstances had brought him down into my world once more had clearly driven him to a little of both.

"Interesting," I murmured, sucking my freshly split open lip into my mouth. "Let me guess... someone took your kid?"

Luca's teeth ground together and the fresh surge of grief and rage in his eyes was all the confirmation I needed. His fist reared back, but a hand caught his wrist before he could deliver the next blow that probably would have split my

Chapter 6

skull open. It wasn't in the best condition after the guard had done a number on it.

I looked over Luca's shoulder to find Silas standing behind him, his posture relaxed and his expression blank as he held his brother-in-law back.

"That's enough," Silas said calmly.

"Fuck you," Luca spat, trying in vain to shirk out of his grasp. "It's not your kid this freak has taken."

"No. It isn't," Silas said quietly. "But I care about Timothy, too. And if you can't believe that, you know Enzo loves him, so you should at least believe I'll do whatever it takes to get Timothy back for Enzo's sake."

Luca said nothing, but even though he was still glowering at Silas, he seemed to be considering his words.

"This isn't the way," Silas continued. "If he does have something to do with this, trust me, torture isn't the way to get it out of him. And in the state he's in now, one more blow is all it'll take for permanent brain damage to set in. He would be useless to us then."

I gave a dry laugh. "Touching."

"You. Silence," Silas hissed, giving me a look that could curdle milk.

"He's right," said Malcolm. "No offense, Luca—you don't have what it takes to get answers out of that fucker. But I do. Let us handle it, and I guaran-fucking-tee I'll get your money's worth."

Luca looked between them, still fuming, but when Malcolm offered his hand, he jerked his arm out of Silas's grasp and let the other man haul him to his feet. He cast a murderous glance at me over his shoulder before walking out of the cell.

Silas grabbed the back of my chair and hauled it into an upright position, making the world spin around me. There were three of him at present, but the middle one was a little sturdier than the others as he stood in front of me, his hands in his pockets as he stared down at me, cold and calculating as ever.

"You know, when a kid goes missing, it's usually the other parent," I said, swallowing a mouthful of my own blood. I wasn't sure if it was from inside or outside at this point. "You might have better luck starting there, considering I don't have a fucking clue what you're on about. Unless you're just that desperate for an excuse to see me again."

"It's not the mother," Silas said firmly. "We're sure of that. And if I thought you were directly involved, we'd be having a very different conversation."

"Is that so?" I sneered. "Who knows? Maybe I'm lying."

Silas's expression didn't shift. "It wasn't you," he said in a tone of certainty.

"And what makes you so sure of that?" I challenged.

"I've spent countless hours analyzing your psychological profile," he answered. "First when I was hunting you. Then when I was trying to decide whether you'd be useful as an apprentice. I know every twisted avenue and every dark, filthy corner of your mind, James, and if there's one thing you're not capable of—one line even *you* would never cross —it's harming a child. As a matter of fact, that's always been your trigger, hasn't it? The men you hunted—early on, at least—all had one thing in common. They were predators."

I snorted, turning away from him. "So I have a killing type. Don't we all?"

"That depends on whether the 'we' you're referring to are serial killers," Silas said dryly. "In any case, I'm not here because I think you did it. But I think you have an idea of who might have."

"And why is that?" I asked boredly. While I usually wouldn't turn up my nose at a visit from Silas, the last round of guard duty had left me drained and I really wasn't enjoying the company. I wanted his undivided attention, not an audience.

"Because he asked for you," Luca said through his teeth. There was no mistaking the accusation in his tone, and if what he said was true, he'd be a fool not to jump to that assumption.

"Oh?" Now I was curious.

"There was a ransom note," Silas said pointedly. "Whoever took Timothy wants to make an exchange. The kid for you."

"Huh," I said.

Fresh anger flashed in Luca's eyes, turning them even darker. "This isn't a fucking joke."

"Of course it is," I replied. "And *you're* clearly the punchline."

Luca lunged at me again, but Malcolm grabbed him by the arm to hold him back. "Let me go," Luca snapped. "You hear him? He's clearly got something to do with this."

"He wouldn't be that transparent if he did," Silas said with a weary sigh before turning back to me. "But I do believe he has an idea of who is behind it. And I don't think I need to tell you, James, but whoever is on the other end of this isn't interested in your freedom."

"I've got my share of enemies," I conceded. "Plenty of them who started out as yours. And you say we have nothing in common."

Silas snorted something close to a laugh. Close for him, anyway. "Be that as it may, there are only so many people who could possibly know you're here. Someone who not only knows who you are, but also that you survived my attempt at putting you down and ended up here."

"That does narrow it down," I agreed.

"Who?" Silas demanded.

I didn't answer right away, mostly because I was trying to run down the list myself. I had been careful in the reinvention of my identity. Meticulously so. There wasn't anyone who should have been capable of knowing I was alive besides him and the guy who'd helped me start over, let alone where I was, and I still didn't know how it was possible. But there was only one person I could think of who might have the means—or the motive—to track me down.

"I told you he's not gonna cooperate," Malcolm said gruffly. "Just because we can't beat the shit out of him doesn't mean we can't get the truth by force." A sadistic grin spread across his lips. "Just need to get a little creative, that's all. Skinning's always a good place to start."

Silas frowned, and I could tell he was about to argue when I spoke up.

"Lewis Capello."

Silas froze before turning to face me. I saw a look of recognition slowly cross his face. "Capello," he echoed. "Why does that name sound so familiar?"

"Because his brother Efisio tried to hire you ages ago," I answered. "It was right after you took me in."

Silas blinked at me as if I had said something incomprehensible. "Took you in," he scoffed. "I suppose that's one way to put it."

"You know who this guy is?" Malcolm asked.

"Like he says, it was a long time ago," Silas said thoughtfully.

"I thought you were supposed to have a photographic memory," Luca muttered.

"Eidetic," Silas corrected him in a defensive tone. "And I consume such vast quantities of information to perform my work, I have to discard anything that's irrelevant." He turned back to me. "I turned him down as a client. Why?"

"Because he works in the one industry of the underworld even you won't stain your hands with," I answered pointedly.

A dark look came into Silas's eyes. I knew it well. Disgust mingled with pure, murderous rage. It was a more muted version of what I felt, but everything was when it came to him. Everything but the obsession he felt for his pet mobster.

It was one of the reasons I'd remained loyal to him all these years. Even now, whether he saw it that way or not. There were few monsters who still maintained a sense of honor, even if it was only one they had cobbled together for themselves.

"They sell children," he muttered, his lips curling over the words in disgust.

"On a scale that would make the devil vomit," I answered. "Of course, they were more of a small-time operation back then, but Lewis has taken the family business to new depths of depravity. And infamy. Even back then, they had enough friends in high places that you couldn't just take them out like you did with most of the people of their ilk who were foolish enough to darken your door."

"It's coming back to me," Silas said. "I seem to recall a certain senator who was intimately connected with the family."

"Oh, they're still quite cozy last I heard," I assured him. "Among others."

"I told you not to mess with them," Silas said, his eyes narrowing. "You disobeyed me."

"The one and only time," I said pointedly. "But if you actually expected me to listen, you have only yourself to blame. Like you said. I have a type."

"You killed him," Silas said, pinching the bridge of his nose. "You killed Efisio."

"I waited an appropriate length of time after you refused him service," I said.

Chapter 6

"Obviously not long enough if Lewis found out it was you," Silas hissed. "And you never told me."

"What, so you could decide I was compromised and take me out?" I challenged.

He didn't deny it.

"Wait a second," Malcolm said, holding up his hand. "You're telling me you would have taken your own asset out because he killed that perv?"

"I wasn't aware of what he'd done," Silas said darkly. "But I would have, yes. I can't afford to have wildcard vigilantes working for me."

"Unbelievable," Malcolm muttered. I knew better than to think it was out of pity for me rather than anger toward his brother, of course. His hatred of me was the one thing I couldn't really fault him for, after I'd killed his first husband and kidnapped the second.

"He took me out for other reasons shortly after that, anyway," I said bitterly. "Just business. Isn't that right, Silas?"

"You stayed dead," Silas said, ignoring my question. "Were you hiding from me? Or from Lewis?"

"Both," I answered with a shrug. "In the end, it worked out. At least, it did for a while. Staying dead requires an active investment of time and resources, and it would seem you haven't been as careful about covering my tracks as I was."

Silas glared at me with that stone cold stare, but he didn't say anything.

"So you're telling me human traffickers have my kid?" Luca demanded, sounding freshly panicked.

"Lewis isn't like his brother," I said, even though I had no idea why I felt compelled to reassure a man who'd just cold clocked me. "It's not personal for him. It's just business."

"That's really not comforting," Luca snapped.

"Maybe not," I said with a shrug. "But if he's done this, he won't hurt the kid until he gets what he wants."

"And after that?" Luca pressed.

I stared at him for a few moments, knowing I had to choose my words carefully around the others. Especially Malcolm. "Let's just say if you hand me over, you're not getting him back. That's not how Lewis works. No honor among thieves and all that."

"Bullshit," Malcolm growled. "If he's doing this to get revenge on his brother, and Silas had nothing to do with his death, I say we hand your ass over, get the kid, and then blow you all to kingdom come. Not like anyone would miss you."

"Do you really think he isn't counting on that?" I asked. "You think he hasn't planned out every contingency? He knows you'll double-cross him, and Lewis didn't get to where he is by leaving loose ends. That's exactly what Timothy will be once you hand me over to Lewis, and there's nothing left protecting him. I'm the only person who's ever infiltrated the organization deep enough to know how to extract him safely. Like it or not, you need me, and if you use me as a hostage exchange, all your leverage and intel is gone. Just like that. And *you*," I said, turning to Luca, "can say goodbye to any hope you have of ever seeing your son again."

Luca met my gaze, his dark and unreadable. There was more mettle behind it than I'd given him credit for, but every man had his limits. And I could tell he was a hair's breadth away from his.

"You don't have to take my word for it," I said, keeping my focus on him since I knew Silas was already thinking ten steps ahead, and Malcolm simply wasn't worth reasoning with. "I'll prove to you that I know exactly what I'm talking about. Within the next twelve hours or so, Lewis will contact you again from an untraceable VOIP number using a VPN. The call will probably be routed through Barbados, but possibly Bermuda. He won't let you speak to your son, but ask anyway. It's part of the game. He'll tell you he wants to speak to me next time in exchange for hearing your son's voice. Maybe a picture. I suggest you agree to his terms—assuming the demands of single fatherhood haven't become too much."

Luca's eyes narrowed dangerously. For a second, I thought he was going to attack me again. Instead, he turned to Silas. "Do you trust him?"

"Absolutely not," Silas answered without hesitation. "But I don't think he's lying in this case. So we'll just have to wait and see."

7

LUCA

The next call came around ten hours after the first, just as James said it would. Silas and Malcolm already had a setup at the family home to trace the call as soon as it came through.

Time seemed to stand still as the phone rang. I looked up at Silas, who nodded for me to take the call.

"Good evening, Luca," the man on the other end of the line said before I had the chance to even answer. His voice was low and smooth, and there was something about it that made me sick. The fact that this man was the one who had my kid was enough to drive me out of my mind.

"Lewis," I said through my teeth.

"Ah, very good," he said. "I see your brother-in-law figured it out already. I assume he's there? And tracing the call, no doubt. That's perfectly fine. I don't have an abundance of time to chat, but I'll be sure to stay on long enough he can get a connection. Protocol and all that."

Chapter 7

"My son," I said, struggling to keep my anger from choking the words out of my throat. "Where is he?"

"Safe," Lewis said, and I heard the smugness in his voice. "Safe and well distanced from all the unsavory aspects of the family business I'm sure Silas has filled you in on by now. And I give you my word, he'll stay that way as long as you continue to comply with these negotiations."

"And why the hell should I believe you?" I demanded. "Your word doesn't mean shit."

"Fair enough," he conceded. "But we're getting ahead of ourselves. You want to talk to your son, and I want reassurance that Demon is still alive, but I can all but guarantee you haven't been able to convince them to move him from whatever hole he's been hiding in."

I gritted my teeth, torn between relief and frustration that this was all going according to the way James had said it would. A little too closely. "You're working with him," I accused.

"Now that would be a twist, wouldn't it?" Lewis mused. "Alas, I don't think your prisoner holds me in quite the same high esteem as I hold him. But it doesn't really matter, does it? I have something you want, and you have something I want. As long as we're both reasonable about this, there's no reason we can't both be happy."

"When can I talk to him?" I demanded.

"When I feel like it," he answered in a casual tone, as if we were simply two old acquaintances discussing when to meet up for coffee. "Just make sure you're available at night."

My stomach roiled. What the hell kind of game was he playing?

Silas nodded once more, his expression unreadable as he remained focused on the call, a headset over his ears. Malcolm was leaning against the other wall, dead silent, but I could see the wheels turning behind his eyes.

Everyone, including he and Valentine, had moved into the family mansion for the time being, as our new base of operations. But Val was treating a patient and Enzo was out supervising the manhunt. The cops were useless as far as Malcolm was concerned, and the family's enforcers probably weren't going to fare much better at finding this guy if he had managed to track James down despite Silas's best efforts to keep him hidden from the world.

But we still had to fucking try.

I wanted to be out there myself, but logically, I knew I had to be here. I was the only point of contact Lewis seemed like he was willing to deal with at the moment. That didn't stop me from going crazy.

"Fine," I said, sounding a hell of a lot calmer than I was. "He'll be here when you call. But I want to speak to my son first."

"That's not how this game works, Luca," Lewis said in a patronizing tone. "You don't get to make the rules. But I'll tell you what. You've been such a good sport up until now that I'll send you a picture as proof your little angel is just fine. Make sure you keep your end of the bargain and he'll stay that way."

"Wait—" I broke off as the line went dead.

Chapter 7

A few moments later, the phone lit up with a message. There was a picture someone had taken from across the room of where Timothy was sitting on the floor in what looked like a relatively normal living room, playing with a toy train that was identical to the one he had at home. In front of the camera to the right was a newspaper with the day's date on it. He looked relatively happy, all things considered, but the sight of him both filled me with relief and the deepest fear I had ever known.

My boy. They had my boy. He was alive and safe, but for how long?

"This picture," I said, shoving the phone into Silas's hands. "Can you get anything from it?"

Silas hesitated, looking down at the phone. "There are no windows, but there might be some identifying features. I can have a team look at it," he said carefully. "But I'm sure all the metadata is scrubbed, and we're not going to find anything Lewis doesn't want us to find."

He was right. I knew he was, but it was a straw and I was grasping desperately.

"You have to do it," I said, looking pointedly at Malcolm. "He has to be out of there and ready to talk to Lewis by tomorrow night."

Malcolm clearly wasn't happy about it judging from the frown on his face, but he grunted an acknowledgment. "Have him fitted with a collar," he told Silas. "I still think there's a damn good chance he's the one orchestrating all this."

"I don't," Silas said, sounding more certain than he had a right to be. "But we won't take any chances."

That was the one fucking thing I'd ever agreed with him on.

8

JAMES

The guards came to get me right on schedule, and considering the fact that Malcolm and Silas had been sniffing around lately a lot more than usual, they had been on good behavior. Which meant I was getting the royal treatment of not having my face pounded into the cement floor.

Practically a vacation.

Neither man said a word, so I assumed I was getting out. Otherwise, they would have been gloating and rubbing my nose in my impending punishment.

When they brought me to the clinic in the upper ward, I knew it.

I'd been here for treatment on plenty of occasions when the guards deemed my injuries too risky to leave unattended. Not out of concern for my well-being, obviously, but rather fear that their employer would retaliate for damaging his property beyond the point of utility.

The doctor came in without a word, as usual, and Malcolm was soon to follow.

"What a treat," I said dryly as Malcolm stalked into the room like an angry tiger, his eyes filled with murder as they locked on me. "I take it everything happened as I predicted it would."

"Your boyfriend called, all right," he answered. "Guess it's your lucky day. But if you think you're gonna be better off right under my nose than in here, you're not half as smart as you think."

"And here I was looking forward to spending some quality time together," I taunted.

Malcolm blew a puff of air through his nostrils and turned to the doctor. "Use the biggest needle you've got."

The woman didn't say a word, but she eyed me warily as she prepared the microchip. I wasn't sure if it was merely a tracker, or if it possessed some kind of killswitch in case I got out of line, but either way, I knew it was going to sting like a bitch.

Malcolm stood by, watching with a sadistic smile on his face as the needle pierced the back of my neck. It was certainly a few gauges larger than it needed to be. I moaned as they pushed the chip in, but his smile faded when the tenor turned more orgasmic than pained.

"Ooh, that was a good one," I gasped. "How about another? Just to cover our bases. They can reject, you know."

"Now the collar," Malcolm said through his teeth.

Chapter 8

The doctor walked over to a flat black box on a tray in the center of the room that had clearly been specially prepared for the occasion.

"For me?" I asked, turning to Malcolm as she carried the plain silver circlet over to us. "You shouldn't have. What is Val going to think?"

"It's a different kind of collar," he sneered, his arms folded as he stood by watching me. "One that will pump a fatal dose of potassium chloride into your jugular if I press a single button. And you never know, James. I might have sweaty palms with all this shit going on."

"Pretending like you actually care about the little tyke," I said with a chuckle. "That's cute."

His eyes narrowed, but he said nothing as the doctor approached me, appropriately hesitant. She fit me with the collar, and when it locked in place, I felt a mechanism within the metal shift.

"He's all set, sir," the doctor announced, stepping back from the table to put a good distance between us. Smart lady.

Malcolm nodded for me to get off the table. I followed him, willing to play the obedient captive for the time being. Once we were out of the clinic, he traded my cuffs for a set of metal bracers that wrapped from my wrists all the way up my forearms.

"Just a little added security," he said. "But you're smart enough to know it's not necessary, aren't you? And if you try anything, you'd better hope to God someone presses that button before I get to it. Manually."

"Noted," I said with a yawn.

He kept walking, and I followed him to an elevator further down the hall that led up into a massive garage. Once we reached the obnoxiously nondescript black SUV he unlocked with a keyfob, I was entirely unsurprised when Malcolm shoved me into the back of the vehicle and yanked a bag down over my head.

As if I didn't know exactly where the fuckers lived. And which drawers they kept their socks in, for that matter.

He made sure the drive was as bumpy as possible, because of course he did.

The bag didn't come off my head until I was forced into a leather chair that smelled like wood-scented air freshener.

"Love what you've done with the place," I remarked, looking around the DiFiores' living room. "It really gives off Godfather knockoff vibes."

Luca was there, along with Silas, Malcolm, and Enzo, but Valentine was conspicuously absent. I had no doubt Malcolm was protecting his pet from me. As if he hadn't been merely a means to an end.

Which was funny, because I kind of liked him. If only because I found him amusing.

"Glad you like it," Enzo said, his arms folded as he stared down at me. Now there was the man I most wanted to turn into a skin suit. I'd mount him on my fucking wall and make Silas stare at him all day if I could stand decor that tacky. "I guess Malcolm filled you in on why you're here."

"He did, indeed," I said, glancing over at Luca. "I take it he didn't let you speak to your son."

Chapter 8

"No," Luca said, his voice tense and his eyes bloodshot like he'd either been crying, hadn't slept in a week, or both. To his credit, he was handling it better than most people in his position would have. "But the next time he calls, you're going to be here. And you're going to talk to him."

"I will," I agreed. "But you're naive if you think you can send me back to the prison after that. This is just the beginning, and you need my help."

"You're collateral," said Silas. "Nothing more and nothing less."

I scoffed. "Please, Silas. I know you can afford to be lazy now that you're surrounded by people whose idea of an intellectual pursuit is poker night, but put two thoughts behind what you're saying. I'm the only one who knows how the Capellos work, and I'm your best—your *only*—chance at getting the boy back."

Silas's gaze darkened, but I could tell I wasn't telling him anything he didn't already know. "You'll stay here for the time being, and you will cooperate," he said finally. "And I think you know well enough what the consequences will be if you don't."

"Don't get so sensual, love. He'll get jealous," I said, nodding toward Enzo.

Silas rolled his eyes before turning to Luca. "Lewis will be calling on your phone, so I think it would be best if James stayed in your room."

"Is that really such a good idea?" Enzo asked warily.

His trepidation was understandable enough. Luca was the one who detested involvement in the family business in any capacity, and now Silas wanted him to room with a killer.

"We can't afford to waste any time once he calls, love," Silas reasoned. "I have the phone monitored, but Luca needs to be the one to answer, and he'll want to speak to James."

"It's fine," Luca said impatiently. When Enzo seemed about to argue further, he added, "I said it's fine."

"Brave boy," I purred, earning a glare from Silas and Enzo alike.

"Not another word out of you," Silas snapped. "If you know what's good for you, you'll be grateful for every second you're not rotting in that basement and act like you have some sense of self-preservation."

"I'll be on my best behavior," I assured him, smiling at Luca. "In fact, I'm looking forward to it."

9

LUCA

Finding out that fucking Demon was going to be sharing my bedroom at the main house was just par for the course in a day that was already as shitty as possible.

And I didn't buy that he was going to be on "good behavior." Not for a single second—not that I thought his idea of good behavior was anything to have high hopes about to begin with.

"That is where you sleep," I told him, pointing to the iron cage on the other side of the room. It had been Malcolm's idea, and while it was far from an ideal solution, it beat having a fucking serial killer with free rein in my room while I was trying to sleep. I only managed a few minutes here and there as it was, and I needed to stay sharp, because the last thing I wanted to do was fumble the next phone call that psycho made.

"Kinky," he sneered, slinking around the edge of the bed to sit down on the corner. "You don't trust me?"

"No," I answered. "I don't."

"Pity. We could have so much fun."

I opened the door to the cage and stood aside pointedly. "Get in."

He sighed, getting up to walk over to it. "You really are the boring one."

I held up the remote Malcolm had given me. "There's a button on here that will light your ass up. So think twice before you get any ideas."

"A shock? Is that all?" He made a clicking sound with his tongue. "Malcolm has the one that will administer a lethal injection. He must not trust you with the grown-up toys."

I narrowed my eyes. He was trying to get to me, and it was easier to do that than I wanted to admit, but my nerves were already frayed, so I was going to give myself some slack in that department. "Cage. Now."

He rolled his eyes, but he sank to his knees and got in, which admittedly looked difficult with his arms bound in those giant metal bracelets. I wasn't really sure what he could do even if he did get out of the cage, but his reputation left me unwilling to let my guard down at all. Something told me that would end up being a mistake I might not live to regret.

A few hours into the night, I learned that James moaned in his sleep—and dreamed about Silas. They didn't sound like particularly pleasant dreams, either.

Chapter 9

Of course, I had no way of knowing if that was just another act or not, and it was safe to assume everything was with him.

My phone rang in the middle of the night. I realized I must have actually fallen asleep when I jolted out of a nightmare and found it in my lap.

When I saw it was Carol's number, my heart at once sank and filled with relief.

"Carol," I muttered, rubbing my face. It was well after one in the morning, so I was surprised she was calling.

At least until I heard how slurred her voice was.

"Have they found him?" she asked.

I felt my gut tighten immediately.

"No," I said, since that was technically the truth. "They haven't, but the police are looking. So are we."

No matter how shitty things had been between me and Carol, and regardless of whether she wanted to be or not, she was still the mother of my child and I still felt like shit for lying to her. I felt like shit for everything, but there was only so much I could tell her without risking further complications that might jeopardize the operation.

Silas and Malcolm had already been clear that the fewer details she knew, the better, and telling her about the ransom note would unravel the thread of secrets my brothers-in-law were keeping, which would put a bounty on her head, too. And it wouldn't be just Lewis I had to worry about protecting her from. It would be Silas and Malcolm, too.

"It doesn't make sense," she said, her voice strained from crying. "How could someone just take him? There are rules. He was supposed to be safe. You were supposed to keep him safe, Luca."

Her words and the pain in her voice felt like a gut punch. "I know," I said, my voice thick with emotion I couldn't let myself feel in full right now. The moment I did, it was all going to unravel.

My composure. Me. Everything.

"I'm sorry, Carol. I don't know what else to say."

"You should be," she seethed, her voice turning venomous in an instant. "This is your fault. You let this happen. To punish me."

"What the hell is that supposed to mean?" I asked, my voice louder than I'd intended. The last thing I wanted was to have an audience for this conversation. Especially James, but privacy wasn't a luxury I could afford right now. "You think I lost our son because I'm angry at you for leaving?"

"I don't know," she said, her voice breaking as she sounded less certain. "Maybe. For leaving, and for not being the wife and mother you wanted me to be."

My throat tightened and I took a deep breath. "You're drunk, Carol. Try to get some sleep."

"Stop it!" she hissed. "That's the shit you always say. God, you sound like a broken record. It's always me, isn't it? I'm always out too late, drinking too much, not paying enough attention to Timothy. Nothing is ever good enough for the perfect Luca DiFiore. Like you're some fucking saint."

Chapter 9

"I never said I was a saint," I murmured.

"You didn't need to say it. It's in your eyes. It's in the way you and everyone else have always acted, even my parents," she snapped. "'Oh, he's such a good guy. You're the perfect couple.' It's fucking exhausting having to be perfect all the time. Having the whole world think you're happy when you're miserable. I tried so hard to love you. I really fucking did, but I don't. And you know what? I never did, but everyone else loved you so fucking much, I convinced myself I did, too."

Another gut punch. Even if it was nothing I didn't already suspect. Nothing I hadn't heard whispered in that still, small voice in the back of my mind all those nights I lay awake next to a woman who acted like touching me was a chore for the latter half of our marriage. "I'm sorry," I said once I trusted myself to speak. "I'm sorry being married to me was so difficult. I thought I was being a good husband."

"You were," she said, her voice raw with emotion. Pain. Pain that I had caused, apparently, just by existing. "But it wasn't enough. It just... it isn't, and I couldn't do it anymore. I thought I'd finally gotten away, and I could be free, and then this..."

She trailed off, but her implication was clear enough. "I'm sorry our son's disappearance is so inconvenient for you," I gritted out. "But I will bring him back. I'm bringing him home, and in the meantime, I suggest you think long and hard about whether you actually want to be a part of his life. Because the in and out shit? He deserves better than that. He deserves better than either of us."

"Go to hell, Luca."

"Go to sleep, Carol," I muttered, hanging up.

I buried my face in my hands, taking a deep breath to calm down. When I looked up, James was watching me silently from across the room, no expression at all on his face.

"That was rough," he remarked.

"Sorry to disturb your sleep," I said, reaching into my bedside table for a bottle of scotch I hadn't let myself touch in months. Until the last couple of days, at least. I poured a shot glass and downed it, since that was the only way I was going to get any more sleep. I wasn't going to take any pills and risk not waking up if that phone rang again.

"The missus sounds like a real treat," he said. "I can see why things worked out so well."

"Don't," I said in a warning tone. "Not a word about her. Not out of you."

"How chivalrous," he sneered. "I'm starting to see what she means, though. The white knight routine would get old after a while."

I turned over to face the door, planning on ignoring him for the rest of the night.

"You know," he said after it had been long enough I'd assumed he had given up on fucking with me and gone back to sleep. "You can make good on that promise you made her. If you do what I tell you, you'll get your son back."

"You're not the one calling the shots here," I said pointedly. "But even if you were, why the hell should I believe you'd want to help me do anything? Why should I believe you care about anything other than yourself?"

"You shouldn't," he answered. "But I loathe loose ends, too, and Lewis Capello is certainly one of them. That, and it wouldn't hurt Silas's opinion of me."

I snorted. Given his obsession with Silas, that checked out.

He was right, though. If he'd pretended to be helping for selfless reasons, I wouldn't have believed him at all, but that made a little more sense. And if there was one thing I had learned to trust about a psychopath, it was that he would do anything to promote his own self-interest.

Love was no exception.

10

JAMES

I had barely been at the mansion for a day, and already, I had managed to convince Silas it was in his best interest to give me a laptop to work from. It was heavily monitored, of course, but that didn't matter.

I was using it for the stated purpose, at least at this point. I'd been gone for long enough that all the systems I'd had in place to keep tabs on Lewis—and the others who would hunt me relentlessly—were eroded. If we stood a chance at tracking him down, I needed information, even if it meant Silas now had access to at least some of my former networks.

If I played my cards right, we'd be working together and not against each other anyway. The way it should have been from the beginning. The way it was meant to be.

He just didn't see it yet.

I'd tried forcing his hand, and that had failed spectacularly. I was crazy, but not so crazy I was going to keep trying the

Chapter 10

same failed tactics over and over again until he inevitably killed me. It was time for a new approach.

As I sat at the kitchen table, getting caught up on all things Capello for the last year and a half, there were two armed guards stationed at either entrance. One of them was Johnny DiFiore, Enzo's cousin and a constant thorn in my side, while the other was clearly one of Silas's goons. I'd know the fresh-out-of-Quantico look anywhere.

At least they didn't try to make small talk. Not after the last few times I'd shot down Johnny's attempts at getting under my skin. Silas and Malcolm might have found the low-level mobsters amusing, but I had never been a fan of cheap entertainment.

I was pleasantly surprised, though, when the youngest DiFiore brother came waltzing into the room halfway through the day.

"Valentine," I said in the most pleasant tone I could muster. "Did you slip your leash?"

He frowned. "Chuck broke something and I came over to check on him."

"I'm surprised the ogre lets you out of the house," I remarked. Clearly, it was remiss of him. "Let alone in this one."

"It's my house," he said pointedly, folding his arms.

"So it is." I gestured to the empty chair next to me. He sat in the one at the other end of the table.

Precious.

"I thought you were in a cage," he said, looking at the laptop.

"Only at night. Your brother's kinky like that," I said dryly.

He grimaced. I could tell there was something on his mind. He was as transparent as a jellyfish, and the fact that he was here, likely without Malcolm's knowledge, was proof he was bothered enough by whatever it was to overcome his entirely rational fears.

"This guy," he murmured. "You really think he won't hurt Timothy?"

"Of course he would," I answered. "But he hasn't. Not yet."

"What makes you sure?"

"Like I said, Lewis is methodical. Most men of his ilk are," I answered. "This is all going to play out a certain way, and as long as your husband doesn't get in the way of me or Silas, it'll work out in the end."

"I hope you mean that," he said, holding my gaze.

I leaned in, closing the laptop. "You didn't just come here for Chuck, did you?"

Valentine swallowed audibly, looking away for a second. He was more nervous around me than usual, but not nearly as much as he probably should have been. Naivete always had been his weak point.

That and a piss poor right hook, but who had the heart to tell him?

Chapter 10

"I knew you for such a long time as Chris," he began somberly. "And I'm still trying to come to terms with everything that happened. Everything you did."

"Understandable enough," I mused. He was a DiFiore, and a fragile one at that. Most people would have a hard time getting over being kidnapped and betrayed by someone they thought they could trust, let alone Valentine, who probably cried every time he stepped on a fucking ant.

"How much of it was real?" he asked, a troubled look on his face. He really was like a big puppy. I could tell from the shakiness in his voice he had been working up the nerve to ask that question for a long time, and now, he finally had his chance.

I paused to consider my answer. For some reason, I actually wanted to tell him the truth, even though I doubted he was going to believe it. "Everything but the name."

His brow furrowed. "Seriously?"

"You can believe it or not," I said with a shrug. "But it's the truth. I liked you. None of it was personal."

"You kidnapped me," he said pointedly. "And you were going to kill my brother. I'd say that's pretty damn personal."

"Not for me," I said. "And not for him, either."

Valentine frowned. "Malcolm? Of course it's personal for him. You killed his fucking husband."

"You're in way over your head, kid," I said with a low chuckle. "If you believe nothing else I've ever told you, believe that. You think you can change him? You think loving you is going to make him a better man? All it's going to do is give him a reason to entrench even deeper into the way he's always been. The way he *chooses* to be. And now, he has something to protect. He has an excuse."

Valentine shook his head. "I didn't come here to get a lecture about my relationship."

"No, I imagine Silas, Luca, and Enzo have given you enough of those," I said dryly. "And you're too foolish to listen, so I certainly won't be the one to change your mind. But don't say I didn't try."

He frowned. "Maybe I am foolish. And naive. But I'm going to ask you something anyway."

"Ask away," I said.

"Help us," he pleaded, giving me the full force of the puppy eyes once more. God, maybe Malcolm really was softening. The kid was relentlessly pathetic. "I know you hate us, and you have every right to hate Silas after what he did to you. I'm not saying you were innocent. Neither is he. Hell, none of us are," he muttered. "But Timothy is. He's a kid and he's scared, and I know you know what that's like. You can pretend you only went after men like Efisio because it was convenient, but we both know the truth runs deeper than that."

"You're doing it again, Valentine," I said in a singsong.

He gave me a confused once-over. "Doing what?"

"Seeing what you want to see," I answered. "Romanticizing a monster."

He sighed. "You sound like Malcolm. He thinks always seeing the worst in people means he's realistic about them."

Chapter 10

"At the risk of agreeing with him, it usually does," I told him.

"Maybe. But not always," he insisted. "I've been in this world long enough to know that even people you trust—people you think would never hurt you—are capable of doing terrible things. I mean, look at my dad. Look at you," he said sadly. "But the opposite has to be true, too. Sometimes people who've done terrible things are capable of doing good, too. Capable of surprising you. I don't know if you're one of them, and maybe everything you ever told me really was a lie, but I'm choosing to believe it wasn't. I'm choosing to believe you're more than just a monster, and that you're capable of more than the terrible things you've done. And I'm asking you to bring him home. Please."

I found myself staring at him for a few moments, torn between the dismissive response on the tip of my tongue and the thing inside me that his earnest stupidity had stirred up.

Before I had the chance to decide, Malcolm came stalking into the room, looking like a bull staring down a red cape.

"What the fuck are you doing talking to him?" he snarled, immediately putting himself between me and his puppy.

"Mal, stop," Valentine pleaded. "We were just talking."

"And what the hell is this?" Malcolm demanded, ignoring his protests as he looked at the laptop in front of me. "You on fucking vacation now or something?"

"Silas authorized it," I said, just to see the flash of anger in his eyes.

"Of course he did," Malcolm muttered.

"You want the kid back, don't you?" I asked. "I can't help you find him if I don't brush up on current events. All that time in captivity has almost crippled my information network."

"*Almost*?" Malcolm echoed in disdain, grabbing the front of my shirt and hauling me to my feet.

Oops.

Luca walked into the kitchen, frowning as he took in the scene before him. "Hey," he bellowed, walking over to put himself between us. "Watch it. I need him alive."

"My hero," I said flatly.

Luca gave me a silencing glance over his shoulder. "Get back to the room. Now. We need to talk."

"So commanding," I taunted, gathering the laptop before I slipped past him, thoroughly enjoying the rage in Malcolm's eyes as they tracked me across the room. I stopped in the doorway to give Valentine a smile. "We'll finish this conversation another time. Do visit again. I've always loved our little chats."

Valentine didn't respond, but I could tell from the look on his face he wasn't going to give up on his plea anytime soon. He was just dumb enough to think it might actually work.

The problem was, I wasn't sure myself.

11

LUCA

"What is it you wanted to speak about?" James asked in a tone that made it clear he knew damn well exactly why I wanted to talk to him.

As soon as we were inside the room alone, I shut the door and turned to face him. "He still hasn't called," I muttered. "You said he was going to call last night."

"I said he *might*," he corrected in an infuriatingly casual tone. "Be patient."

I grabbed him by the front of the shirt and shoved him up against the wall until we were face-to-face, my arm pinning his body.

"Patient?" I seethed. "He has my son, and you're telling me to be patient? You and this bastard could be working together, for all I fucking know, laughing at us the whole time."

"I could," he agreed calmly. "But it doesn't matter, does it? You can't do anything to me either way, because you'll never see your son again if you do."

Rage washed over me and I realized I had reared my other fist back, ready to strike.

"Go ahead," he sneered. There was a glimmer in his eyes, as if he was anticipating it. As if he was actually enjoying this. "Hit me."

I had never wanted to do anything more in my fucking life, but not like this. I stepped back, even though my resolve only lasted until he was no longer pinned. Until I could justify it. I wasn't hitting a helpless target.

I took a swing and James dodged it easily enough. He grabbed my arm the next time and shoved me back so hard I stumbled. Then he stepped up and slammed his fist into my gut hard enough to knock the wind out of me. I dropped down to my knees, groaning as pain radiated throughout my body.

"You walked into that one," he said in a bored tone.

I got up and shoved him as hard as I could back into the wall again, but he rushed forward and tackled me, using my own momentum against me.

We both went crashing into the end table, wood splintering as I landed on top of him and wrapped my hands around his neck.

His eyes were alight with something like glee as he clawed at my wrists hard enough to draw blood. He was fucking strong. A hell of a lot stronger than he looked, even though he wasn't quite as bony as he'd been after being released from the prison. He was still capable of feats someone so much lighter than I was shouldn't have been capable of, and when he rolled so he was the one on top of me, I realized I'd let my guard down.

I grabbed the remote, my finger hovering over the shock button. James froze, staring down at me with his hair brushing the tops of my shoulders. I was about to push the button when he did the one thing that could have stopped me.

He kissed me.

All I could do for a few moments was lay there in shock, my eyes wide and unblinking as he crushed his lips against mine.

And rather than push him off, or push the button, or any of the other things that would have made infinitely more sense, I returned the kiss.

I had no idea what the fuck I was even doing, but the aggression our fight had merely fanned into a roaring flame had found another outlet, and I claimed it as fiercely and violently as I had been willing to fight him.

Not that James gave me much of a chance to think or respond rationally. As soon as I began to respond in kind, his tongue flicked against my lips, seeking entrance. Mine parted instinctively and his tongue swept in, silky and slick as it traveled over mine.

I was caught off guard enough by the kiss that the remote slipped from my grasp, and I felt a surge of panic as he reached for it. He simply pushed it across the floor, as if one wrong press couldn't immobilize him.

It had been so long since I'd touched someone like this, and I was surprised by just how much I craved it. Even if it was from another guy.

What the fuck was wrong with me?

Something told me the answer to that question wouldn't fit in a thousand-page book, but I was too pent up with chaotic energy burning beneath my skin and demanding release to care right now.

James was straddling my hips, and he broke the kiss to lean back, grinding his ass against my cock. It stiffened traitorously, but at least I could tell myself it was just the physical sensation and the fact that I hadn't fucked anyone in the better part of a year.

I groaned involuntarily, my hips arching up into him as he started tearing my shirt open, his nails dragging along my bare flesh hard enough to draw blood.

"What are you—?"

"Shh." He pressed a finger to my lips. Like there was any doubt he was a complete fucking creep.

So what did it make me if I was turned on right now?

I grabbed his wrist and pulled his hand away, trying to get back some measure of control. Even if he was the one wearing a collar. "Are you crazy or something?"

"That wasn't abundantly obvious?" he challenged, pushing my hands off and peeling his shirt off over his head. "You really haven't been paying attention."

I rolled my eyes, trying not to study his naked torso. It was just second nature to look at someone getting undressed,

Chapter 11

especially when that someone was aggressively coming on to me, but I'd never looked at another guy that way. Sure as hell not him.

So why was I...?

"Don't think so much," he scolded, climbing off me enough to tug off his jeans. "You'll ruin everything."

"You say that like this is something I wanted in the first place," I muttered. "I'm straight. And in case you haven't noticed, I fucking hate you."

"That makes it all the more fun," he answered. "What's the point of sex without a little hate? It's like a cocktail without alcohol."

"Juice," I said flatly. "They just call that juice."

He rolled his eyes, and started unfastening my belt. "You can't kill me. And as I think I've proven, you can't even fight me without having to resort to means that are counterproductive to you. But you can fuck my brains out, and really, isn't that the next best thing?"

In his own incredibly fucked-up way, he had a point. And maybe that was proof I really was losing my mind, if the homicidal lunatic was starting to make sense to me.

"Fuck it," I muttered under my breath, pushing his hands away to finish the job of freeing my own cock. I pushed him off and adjusted our positions so I was the one on top of him. "If we're doing this, I'm on top."

"No complaints there, handsome," James purred, lying back and spreading his legs enough to allow me between them. "You got lube, or are we doing this the fun way?"

I gave him a wary look, reaching into the bedside table for a condom. "Somewhere in between. No offense, but I'm not fucking you raw."

"None taken," he said, watching boredly as I opened the condom and slid it down over my cock. "Magnum XL. Guess you were packing heat this whole time."

"Do you ever shut up?" I muttered, questioning my decision to fuck him face-to-face since that felt a little too intimate.

And it was a little harder to pretend I wasn't fucking a guy that way, even though my cock at full mast clearly wasn't having any problems with it.

"Would you prefer it this way?" he asked knowingly, rolling onto his stomach with his ass bared to me and his knees spread, his stiff cock bobbing between them.

I froze, unable to take my eyes off him. I'd never experienced so many conflicting emotions in my fucking life. My cock was throbbing painfully as I stared at his round, tight ass and the muscular thighs that were spread apart so invitingly. His strong back arched as I came up behind him, positioning myself between his cheeks, and buried my cock in him in one swift motion.

I really didn't feel like gentleness was something he deserved or was going to tolerate, and to his credit, he took it. His fingers dug into the carpet and his spine arched again as his body clenched down around my cock, squeezing it hard from base to tip.

"Fuck," I gritted out. He was tight. I wasn't sure what I'd expected, but... damn, that kind of hurt.

"What's the matter?" he taunted, his voice slightly strained and husky from the pain, I assumed. "Don't tell me the cheerleader never let you fuck her in the ass?"

"Don't bring her into this," I said through my teeth, gripping a fistful of his hair to brace myself. Just because I was divorced and hadn't been married in any genuine sense of the word for a good while before that didn't mean it was easy to get over the mental hurdles. Not just of being with another guy, but of being with anyone other than my wife.

Something told me if James had any idea what was going through my head, I'd never hear the end of it. And he certainly had more than enough fodder to torment me with as it was.

A pleasured moan escaped him that was far more appealing than it had any right to be. This was about finding an outlet for my anger and burning off some tension. Nothing more and nothing less, and yet as I drove into him, and he seemed to absorb every ounce of aggression and pain like he needed it to survive, I couldn't help but get drawn in.

This was a mistake. Undoubtedly. And I was sure this was just another game he had perfectly calculated and lured me into from the beginning, but knowing that didn't change the fact that I wanted to play.

"You're big," he said, his voice hoarse with desire. "It's always the quiet ones, isn't it?"

I growled, pushing deeper inside him. "We really don't need to talk for this."

"But banter is my turn on," he taunted. "And you're cute when you're angry."

I drove into him at a different angle, and when I heard his strangled cry of pleasure and surprise, I knew I'd succeeded at hitting his prostate. That was one way to shut him up, if nothing else.

I found my hand pressed against his stomach to keep him where I wanted him, my fingers brushing over the sculpted lines of his abs. As I thrust into him from behind, I could feel his muscles flexing beneath my touch, and I was tempted to explore further.

His ass was firm and tight, and his body was lean and muscled, but not overly. My hand drifted down naturally, even though there was no reason for this to be anything more than a quick fuck, and my fingers swept over the patch of short, surprisingly soft hair at the base of his cock. I'd never even thought of touching another man like this, and he hadn't even asked me for it, but I grabbed his cock anyway, stroking him as I thrust harder.

I told myself it was just to feel less guilty for the fact that I was fucking him so aggressively, even though he clearly didn't have a problem with that, either. When he moaned, though, I couldn't justify the way my cock throbbed in response to that sound. There was nothing utilitarian about that reaction.

It was purely instinctive, and I hated myself for it.

Raking myself over the coals for enjoying this wasn't going to change the fact that I was doing it, though, so for the time being, I chose to push my guilt aside and focus on the task at hand.

My balls slapped against his ass with each thrust, and every now and then, he'd clench down on me, pushing me to the

Chapter 11

point where I wasn't sure how much longer I could hold back. I was the one inside him, but he was in control, and he wanted me to know it.

"You like that?" he purred, his voice low and throaty.

"Yes," I said through my teeth, driving into him faster.

He laughed softly, and it sent shivers down my spine. "You know, for a straight guy, you're not that bad. Definitely plenty of raw material to work with."

"Would you just shut up?" I muttered, finding myself draped over him in an attempt to pull him even closer, like I wasn't sheathed balls-deep in his tight ass. My lips brushed against the back of his neck, my breath stirring his hair, and I couldn't resist the strange urge to let my teeth scrape along his skin.

To my surprise, that ignited a chain reaction. His cock twitched in my grip, pulsing with life and arousal as I teased him. The sudden flare of lust was unexpected, but welcome, and it only fueled the fire of my own desire.

I started stroking him harder and bit down on the flesh my teeth had only grazed, and he came with a startled gasp.

"Fuck," he cursed, arching his back and pushing back against me. "Fuck, Luca. You're killing me."

I chuckled and leaned forward to kiss the side of his neck. It was far more intimate than I'd planned on, but it felt right. And wrong. And hot.

My own release was imminent, and I was surprised by how much I wanted it. The fact that I could not only get it up for another guy but come inside him was a testament to how badly I needed this.

But fuck it, I did. And as I came inside him, his body still clenching down on mine as he rode the ripple effects of his orgasm, I couldn't even tell myself it was going to be the last time.

Not if it felt this fucking good.

12

JAMES

I woke up aching in places I had forgotten existed, yet feeling thoroughly refreshed. I moaned in blissful agony as I rolled over to an empty bed.

Luca was gone, of course.

I got out of bed and yawned, limping my way into the shower. The hot water was at once pleasurable and agony on my battered muscles and torn flesh.

I had marks from his nails all over my body, and as I washed the last traces of blood from my legs and cheeks, I felt the sting of the water inside me, too, calling back memories of the night before.

I had to admit, there was more to Luca than I'd thought. He was brutal in bed, which had always been my definition of a good lover. What he lacked in skill from never having been with a man before could definitely be made up for in practice.

Now that I had reason to believe he was open to more experiences outside his comfort zone, maybe this wasn't going to be such a dull tenure, after all.

Once I had sufficiently cleaned up, I got dressed and headed downstairs. When I saw that Enzo was alone in the kitchen, I felt like I'd struck gold.

It really was my lucky day.

"Oh. You," he said, glancing up from the ungodly amount of eggs and bacon he was frying up in the same skillet, like some kind of wildebeest with thumbs. He squinted. "You look rough. And are you limping? Val said Luca stopped Malcolm from beating the shit out of you."

"He did," I said, going over to the coffeemaker to pour myself a cup of burnt bean juice that tasted like a walnut's ass. It was caffeine, though, and for a family that had made its fortune off illicit trades, there was a notable shortage of cocaine in the DiFiore household.

"Hungry?" Enzo offered.

I narrowed my eyes. "I'd rather die. Thanks."

"You're fine drinking my coffee," he said pointedly, turning off the stove.

"You call this coffee?"

"More for me, then," he said with a shrug.

Silas walked into the room while Enzo was still getting out the dishes and barely glanced my way before walking over to the other man. "Morning, love."

Chapter 12

I watched as he took Enzo into his arms and kissed him breathless. Disgust mingled with a deep, clenching pain in my gut as I watched him hold another man the way he'd once held me, but even though I knew the kiss was at least partly to mark his territory, there was more passion behind it than he'd ever shown me.

I ground my teeth, trying to bite back my rage. When Silas's eyes met mine, filled with challenge, I masked it and turned away.

"The hell was that for?" Enzo asked breathlessly, his hands resting on Silas's chest like he didn't quite trust himself to stand.

"I need a reason to kiss my husband?" Silas retorted.

I had seen enough. I turned and walked out of the room, because if I didn't, I was going to snap. I'd barely made it down the hall before I lost what remained of my willpower and put my fist through the wall just below the family photos, sending one crashing to the floor.

My adrenaline was still pumping, my fist embedded in the plaster, when I realized my collar hadn't gone off in response to the outburst and my head was still connected to my shoulders.

Good to know that if they were watching me from the cameras I was sure were hidden everywhere, losing my temper wasn't a fatal mistake.

13

LUCA

I'd been out most of the day because I really didn't want to be around James after... whatever the fuck last night had been. But I didn't want to be far, either, and I went home a few hours before sundown just in case Lewis decided to call early.

In the end, my avoidance proved to be for nothing because while James had been sitting at the desk in my room working when I got back, he hadn't so much as glanced up from his laptop for the last two hours.

He had been strangely melancholic ever since I'd gotten back, and while it went against my better judgment to ask why, I couldn't help but wonder if it was because of what had happened last night.

Even though he'd been more than enthusiastic while it was happening, I had been rougher than I'd ever been with anyone. Sure, he seemed to crave that, and he absorbed pain like a fucking sponge, but what if I'd gone too far and hurt him in a way he didn't like during the chaos?

Chapter 13

The thought was enough to make me feel sick, even if a mental rewind of the night before didn't yield any answers. Not unless I had seriously fucking misread things.

"You okay?" I asked, knowing full well I'd probably be given plenty of reason to regret it.

"Why wouldn't I be?" he asked without looking up, scrolling through what looked like a spreadsheet on his laptop.

Yeah, something was definitely wrong. And for all I knew, this was another part of his manipulation, but it was a risk I was willing to take because the alternative was worse.

"*Something* is wrong," I answered, knowing I had to choose my words carefully. "Look, if this is about what happened last night... If I did something wrong..."

He finally looked up, frowning in confusion. "What?"

The sharp tone in his voice made me second-guess my initial assumption of what this was about.

"Uh. I just thought maybe you were having second thoughts about it," I answered. "Or maybe I was too rough?"

His expression went blank, and while the shift in his gaze was subtle, it left me feeling like a subhuman idiot. Like a rat being looked down on by a god. "We fucked," he said flatly. "It's not that deep."

"Right," I said, raking a hand through my hair. "Okay, so if it's not me, what is it? It's pretty clear something got to you."

Irritation flashed in his eyes, but he turned back to his screen. I could tell from the way he was working his jaw that he was far from focused on whatever the hell he was working on, though. "Nothing is wrong. Silas is just finding new and creative ways to punish me."

"Oh," I said, no closer to understanding what was wrong than before. But if it involved Silas, that was probably for the best. "You... wanna talk about it?"

"No," he said in a clipped tone. "I don't want to talk about it. And certainly not with you."

"Jeez," I muttered. "Fine. It was just an offer."

"Worry about yourself," he added in a tone of pure contempt. Yet another side of James. I could swear the guy had more than one personality, and not a single one of them was pleasant.

Not unless you counted the glib, superficially charming creep I'd encountered my first time at the prison, but I'd take bitchy, contemptuous James over that any day. At least I didn't feel like he was going to cut my face off or anything.

"I'm good, thanks," I said, taking out my laptop as I sat against the headboard and decided I might as well get some more work done, since we clearly weren't getting anywhere with this conversation.

"Are you?" he challenged, his tone suspiciously pleasant. "Because this is right about when I'd imagine the guilt is setting in."

Don't bite, the voice of reason inside my head chided.

Of course, I didn't listen. "Guilt? Guilt over what?"

"Guilt for letting your kid get swiped right under your nose?" he offered. "Guilt for letting your own marriage crash and burn? Guilt for being relieved deep down because you don't actually want to be a parent?"

My initial response was to lash the fuck out, especially after that last one, but strangely, having a button in my pocket that went straight to his collar made it easier to hold my temper where he was concerned. And I knew he was trying to get under my skin, so that would just be giving him what he wanted anyway.

"You're right. I do feel guilty," I said. "My marriage was shit, and I've had to own the fact that I had a big part to play in that. And yeah, of course I feel guilty over the fact that I couldn't protect my son. But not wanting to be a parent? That's bullshit. Just because there are rough days doesn't mean you don't love your kid."

"Whatever you need to tell yourself," he snorted.

That was it. I set my laptop aside and stood up, walking over to the desk. "What the hell is your problem?" I demanded.

"I don't have a problem," he said, looking boredly up at me as he leaned against the back of his chair. "I just don't see the point in lying to yourself. But that does seem to be a habit with your family. Case in point, Enzo thinking a block of ice in human form is capable of love, and Valentine thinking he can tame a soulless beast who's bound to eat him alive sooner or later. Then there's you," he sneered. "Daddy dearest, who can't even admit there's a part of him that's relieved his responsibilities are gone."

"You don't know shit," I said, resisting the urge to deck him then and there. Guy or not, hitting someone I'd fucked was crossing an invisible line, and I'd already tap-danced over enough of those where James was concerned. "For the record, I don't trust either of those fuckers any further than I could throw them, and I think both of my brothers have lost their damn minds, but I've been around Silas long enough to know that he does love my brother. At least as much as he's capable of loving anyone. Certainly more than he ever loved you."

I knew I'd struck a nerve as soon as the words were out of my mouth, but it wasn't the anger in his eyes that caught me off guard.

It was the pain.

Something I hadn't even thought he was capable of feeling, and certainly not in response to something that seemed so blatantly obvious to me.

This man was literally a criminal mastermind. A genius. Could he really be so clueless as to believe he actually still stood a shot at winning Silas's heart? A heart I was pretty sure had only ever come into existence because my brother was the one who held it?

It was at that moment I realized James wasn't the cold, calculating monster Silas had tried to mold him into. He wasn't even a rage-fueled, sadistic psychopath like Malcolm. He was human with all the irrational trappings that came with it, each one dialed the fuck up to eleven. And he was all the more dangerous for it.

The hurt lasted only a split second before the anger consumed it, but this time, when he lunged at me, I was ready for him.

I caught him by the wrists before he could deck me, strangle me, or whatever the fuck else he had planned, and this time,

Chapter 13

I was prepared for the amount of force it would take to hold him back.

He was a lot easier to manage when I wasn't underestimating him physically. And his anger seemed to have made him sloppier, too.

"Are you fucking suicidal?" I asked, staring at him in disbelief.

The rage burning in his eyes answered my own question. He might well have been that, too, and I wouldn't have been surprised. But more than anything, he was completely and totally out of control. He didn't simply possess emotions, he was possessed *by* them.

That realization should have been the biggest red flag on the planet, and it was. But it also made me all the more intrigued.

Yeah. Crazy definitely ran in the family.

"Calm down," I gritted out, pushing forward to catch him off balance since he was damn close to gaining the upper hand, and I really didn't want to have to push the not-quite-nuclear button. Not only was it going to render him useless if Lewis called again in the next few minutes, but it was going to make me feel like shit.

"Fuck you," he spat, lunging again with what felt like all his strength.

I pushed back, pinning him against the wall by both wrists. I realized only then I'd been actively trying not to hurt him, but if I didn't get a handle on this situation fast, it was going to escalate to the point of danger for us both.

James froze and stared at me, his eyes widening slightly as if he hadn't expected that.

"*Calm down*," I repeated, holding his stare. I'd found those eyes equally intense when we first met, but they didn't seem cold anymore. More like they were filled with a fire so intense it was hard to tell if I was being burned, but it was hard to look away from them for a myriad of reasons. "Just breathe."

He gritted his teeth, snarling at me like a cornered animal, but he stopped pushing against me like all the fight in him had disappeared. Then he lunged forward again, only this time, rather than fists, he attacked me with a kiss that was just as violent.

Well, that was one method of deescalation.

I kept his wrists pinned and pushed my knee between his thighs, forcing my tongue into his mouth. His lips parted wider, but something sharp pierced my tongue, like he had fucking fangs.

"Ow, fuck," I hissed, breaking the kiss and bringing a hand to my mouth. When I pulled my hand away, my fingertips were stained in red.

"Pussy," James taunted.

I felt a surge of irritation and lust, two things I had once thought were mutually exclusive, and grabbed him by the shirt, tossing him back onto the bed.

"If we're doing this, we're doing it in the bed," I muttered, taking off my shirt as I climbed in between his legs. "I still have rug burn on my knees from last time."

Chapter 13

James sat up to unbuckle my belt and tugged my pants down along with my boxers. "Are you going to fuck me face-to-face, or do you need me to wear a wig?" he asked mockingly.

I reached out to grab a fistful of his hair and yanked his head back. "I dunno. It's pretty long already."

He closed the distance between us and pressed his lips to mine once more, taking my cock in his hand. It was already shamefully hard as he rubbed his thumb over the tip, spreading the precome beading on it.

"Feeling adventurous?" he asked in a seductive, husky voice, his eyes glimmering with amusement as he bent down and flicked the tip of his tongue against the crown of my cock.

My cock throbbed in response to the featherlight, teasing touch, but one look at my blood staining the corner of his full lips was enough to bring me back to my senses.

"Not that adventurous," I said, pushing him onto his back. I undressed him as eagerly as he'd done with me, trying not to think about the fact that I wanted to see another guy's naked body.

Definitely trying not to think about the fact that it turned me on.

Did it even count as being attracted to men if it was a phenomenon entirely specific to one person?

I really hoped the answer was no, because I'd had enough self-revelations through the last year for a lifetime, but at the moment, I couldn't bring myself to care all that much. Instead, I pushed his legs open and reached into the drawer, too desperate to bother with a condom but not quite sadistic enough to want to take him without anything. I grabbed the bottle of lube and smoothed a thick coat of it down my throbbing shaft.

James rolled his eyes. "Aren't we precious?"

"Shut up," I growled, lowering my body onto his to capture his lips if only to keep him quiet. Not that I found his sharp tongue entirely unappealing, if I was being honest with myself.

He returned the kiss eagerly enough, drawing his knees up to grant me better access. I probably should have at least prepared him with my fingers, but he clearly wanted this as much as I did, and I got the feeling he wasn't used to taking things slow.

I just wasn't sure if that was a matter of his preference, or the kind of men he was used to fucking.

His fingers dug into my shoulders as I positioned myself at his hole, and his nails bit into my flesh, drawing blood once again as I breached him.

"Fuck," I hissed.

"Don't be such a bitch," he scolded against my lips, arching his hips to take my cock in deeper as if in consolation.

Or maybe just to shut me up.

"You know, I really can't tell if you get off on feeling pain or inflicting it," I said, adjusting once more to the feeling of being inside him, even if it was only just barely past the crown.

Chapter 13

"Both," he admitted nonchalantly, shifting his position a little beneath me. "Mostly the former, but for you, I'd make an exception."

"I'm flattered," I said dryly, thrusting until I was halfway inside him. Now that we were face-to-face, I had a perfect view of him wincing slightly and as ashamed as I was to admit it, that was definitely a point in favor of this position over the other. Not that I minded getting an eyeful of his perfect ass. The view was ideal either way.

"Less talking, more fucking," he panted, grabbing me by the shoulders to pull me in closer as his hips surged into me once more, taking my cock in the rest of the way.

A strangled moan escaped me as I sheathed myself in him and started rocking my own hips as the friction became more pleasurable than uncomfortable.

This was... fuck, it was good.

It was rough and raw and passionate, and there was freedom in the fact that there was nothing fragile about the man beneath me.

Not physically, at any rate.

Even though I could tell it hurt, the pain seemed to turn him on all the more, and the sight of the pleasure on his face was turning me on more than it had any right to.

Then there was the deep, pulsating satisfaction of being buried inside him, thrusting in and out of his tight passage until I could hardly even keep track of my thoughts.

I found myself reaching for his cock once more, timing my strokes to my thrusts as I drove into him. I knew each time

I'd hit his prostate from the way his eyes darkened and his body tensed around mine.

It didn't just feel good to fuck him, it felt good to pleasure him. To have some measure of control, even if it was only making him moan in bliss.

As rough as it was, there was something about this time that felt different. Like he was more vulnerable somehow. I wasn't sure why that mattered to me, but it did.

Maybe it was just a reminder that the man beneath me was human, despite all the tangled barbed wire he'd wrapped around himself to hide it.

James's fingers slipped into my hair, his gaze darkening as he pulled me in for another kiss. I moaned as his teeth scraped my bottom lip and he bit down gradually enough that I was lulled into a false sense of security. By the time I felt sharp pain and tasted blood, it was too late to do anything, especially since I was already on the verge of coming.

And that, of all things, pushed me over the edge.

"Mmh," James murmured against my lips, his arms wrapping tightly around my neck to pull me in so he could suck on the flesh he'd just broken.

I finally broke the kiss as I filled him with my come, only to see his tongue flicker against my bottom lip, painted in red. The droplets clung to his lips as they parted in an orgasmic gasp, and he arched his back, coming even harder than he had the first time.

"You're out of your fucking mind," I growled, still reeling from the combination of pleasure and pain.

His eyes fluttered open, lit with bliss and malevolence. A combination that had no right to be as beguiling as it was. "You came, though."

I gritted my teeth, pulling out of him without any great care. All things considered, I didn't feel too bad about it.

The most annoying part was, he had a point.

14

JAMES

I slept like the dead that night. At least, I had always assumed that was the only time I would feel anything resembling the peace I felt in that moment, wrapped up in the strong arms of a man my unconscious brain was using as a stand-in for another.

The man whose cold, unfeeling eyes stared back at me in every dream and every nightmare. There really wasn't a difference between them for me, and there never had been. Not when he was present.

I found myself back in that room. So cold and minimalist. A perfect representation of the man who owned it, just like the rest of the penthouse apartment was.

Silas never stayed in one place for long. A few weeks at a time, sometimes months at the most. He alternated safe houses like rich kids alternated their daddies' cars, and for all the luxury that surrounded him, every surface was utilitarian and bare. Utterly devoid of character or personal sentiment. Just the way he liked it.

Chapter 14

I knew, even as I opened my eyes and smelled his expensive Parisian cologne, it was a dream. A lie. It always was, and I might not know which way this one was going to pan out—dream or nightmare—but I was along for the ride all the same.

When I looked up, he was there, looking like a god in repose. He stared down at me, his frigid silver eyes drifting over me so appraisingly. Even in a dream, they couldn't be gentle.

But that wouldn't be real. It wouldn't be him, and I had always loved Silas for exactly what he was. Every jagged edge and sharpened barb that cut into me so deeply and without remorse. It didn't matter, because he filled the holes he left in me with his presence, as fleeting and conditional as it was.

"You talk in your sleep."

It was an offhand remark, and not the first time he'd made it. He was always casually observing and assessing. Adding every bit of data to his repertoire to be used against the subject of his study at a later time, and I was no exception, but I didn't care. I didn't care that I was a set of data points to him, as long as he *was* observing me. As long as he saw me as something.

The sound of ringing jolted me awake much too soon, but when I found myself wrapped up in someone's arms, I felt a surge of hope that maybe this time, it was real.

Then I opened my eyes and realized it wasn't him. It was Luca. I had never despised him more than I did in that moment, and for something so ridiculous. For the crime of not being *him*.

It wasn't like Luca wanted me, either. I was a distraction to him. Last night, I was a charity case. I had known it from the moment I'd seen that look of pity in his eyes, and I knew when I'd attacked him, fucking me had been his way of keeping me in line. His way of keeping me under control so he didn't have to push that button and activate my collar.

And yet, I'd gone along with it. Eagerly, in fact.

I hated myself for that so much more than I could ever hate him.

Luca wasn't waking up fast enough, so I grabbed the phone off the bedside table and put it in his hands. Maybe it was a symptom of whatever the hell was wrong with me that I could wake up and be fully conscious and functional the same instant, but it had its perks.

"It's Lewis," I said, not even having to glance at the caller ID to know that much.

That sobered him up.

"Hello?" Luca answered immediately, his voice steadier than most men's would have been in his situation.

I could already hear footsteps upstairs. Silas's monitoring system was working, and the call was undoubtedly being tapped already, for all the good that would do us. But if Lewis was calling this early, that was a good sign.

It was progress.

"Mr. Capello will speak with you now," said the woman on the other end of the line. I didn't recognize her voice. She was undoubtedly one of his underlings, and probably not

Chapter 14

even in the same building. Hell, I doubted she was even on the same continent.

Luca looked up at me, his eyes wide with panic, but I nodded to reassure him. I grabbed the nearest shirt off the floor, which happened to be his, and pulled it on over my head just as the bedroom door flew open. At least Luca was still in his boxers.

Silas was the first to enter, followed by Enzo, with Malcolm not far behind them. I was used to the subtle shades of shock on Silas's and Malcolm's faces, but with Enzo, there was no hiding it. Just jaw on the floor, eyes wide as saucers.

I raised a finger to my lips to silence him, and turned back to Luca, who looked like he was somewhere between panic and a blind rage.

"Remember what I told you," I said. "Stay calm."

He stared at me for a moment, nodding. A second later, I heard a vaguely familiar voice on the other line.

Silas went to set up with his headset across the desk. I could feel Malcolm watching me like a hawk, until Valentine shuffled into the room after him.

Valentine froze, taking one look at me, then at Enzo, and opened his mouth, but Malcolm clamped a hand over it, pulling the other man against his chest.

"Hello, Luca," said the voice on the other end of the line. It was muffled, but I knew Silas could hear it clearly. "Sorry to call so late, but you know how time zones are."

"My son," Luca said, sounding calmer than I had expected. "Before this goes anywhere else, I need to talk to him."

"In good time," said Lewis. "Did you do what I asked?"

"He's here," Luca said through his teeth.

"Put him on."

Luca looked up at Silas, who nodded, before he passed the phone to me.

"Lewis," I said, keeping my voice devoid of tone. "It's been a long time."

The low chuckle on the other end of the line made my skin crawl. How satisfying it would be to peel his flesh off the muscle, inch by agonizing inch. "Indeed it has. Don't worry. You can wait to thank me for your recently procured freedom in person."

"I can hardly wait," I said flatly. He wanted a reaction, and while I usually would have been happy to give it to him, taking that kind of risk was a bad idea for an abundance of reasons.

The only thing more dangerous than a man motivated by revenge was one motivated by love, and I had to walk a thin line between Luca and Lewis at opposite ends of the spectrum.

"I'm just glad you remembered me," he said, his voice dripping with contempt.

"How could I forget?" I asked. "You've been the ghost on my heels for years now. Out of curiosity, how did you know I was alive?"

"I didn't," he answered. "I never stopped looking just in case, but I didn't know. Not for certain. Not until you stopped

Chapter 14

paying off your contacts. From there, it was just a matter of waiting for the right little fly to step onto my web."

"I see," I said, looking over at Silas. His expression remained blank, but I could tell he'd gotten the point. He had himself to thank. For all of this. "Well, I'm flattered you're still so interested after all this time. Believe it or not, my dance card hasn't been full lately."

"Don't you worry," Lewis scoffed. "Daddy'll give you all the attention you could possibly want soon enough."

Luca nodded toward me, and I could tell he was about to do something stupid, so I pushed forward.

"Sorry to cut the banter short, but I'm going to need you to put the boy on," I said. "This may come as a shock to you, but these men don't seem to trust you very much."

"Imagine that," Lewis taunted. "Too bad you're not the one in charge."

I could tell Luca was about to say something, but I hung up before he had the chance. He went from concerned to livid in a split second, lunging to grab the phone out of my hand.

"What did you do?" he cried, looking down at the phone in horror, his eyes wild with anger and fear as he looked back up at me.

"You son of a bitch," Malcolm seethed, across the room before I could process it. He had me by the throat, pinning me down to the mattress, and his grip was strong enough I started to black out immediately.

"Mal!" Valentine cried in a panic.

"Get your hands off him," Luca snarled, even though he looked like he wanted to do the same. He shoved Malcolm off, putting himself between us.

"It's your kid on the line," Malcolm bellowed. "Are you really so fucking horny you'll defend that piece of shit?"

"He can't fix this if he's unconscious, you fucking moron!" Luca yelled.

"Would you both shut up?" Silas hissed, his eyes locked on me as both men froze. "Care to tell me what the hell that was?"

"Part of the game," I answered, sitting up to rub my throat. My voice was hoarse, but other than being a little lightheaded, there was no harm done.

"Game?" Luca spat, his eyes darkening. "This isn't a game. This is my son we're talking about."

Malcolm gave him an "I told you so" look.

I reached for the phone a split second before it rang, and they all went silent as I lifted it to my ear. Right on schedule.

"Hello?" I answered.

"Daddy?" The small boy's voice on the other end of the line broke, followed by a sniffle.

I held out the phone to Luca as he stared at me in shock. "It's for you."

15

LUCA

As I took the phone from James's hands, I felt a whirlwind of emotions, and I had to compartmentalize and suppress them all or I was going to fall apart. Timothy needed me to be strong and calm, and I was sure he was scared enough.

"Hey, bud," I said, clearing my throat because my voice still sounded rough.

"Daddy!" he cried. "Where are you?"

My stomach clenched like someone had a vice grip on my insides, ready to twist them out of me. "I'm home, but I'm going to come for you real soon. I promise." I knew better than to ask him where he was for a myriad of reasons, not the least of all the fact Lewis would just move him anyway, and possibly retaliate against him. "Are you okay? Are they being nice to you?"

"Yeah." He sniffed. "There are toys and Uncle Lewis is nice, but I miss you."

Uncle Lewis. I gritted my teeth, struggling to see through the blind rage. At least he seemed to be keeping his word, for the time being, and the less afraid Timothy was of him, the better chance he would behave and not do something to anger his captor before I could get to him.

"I miss you, too, kiddo. So much."

"When can I come home?" he asked.

"Soon," I choked out. "Soon, I promise."

"Here. Can I have that?" I heard Lewis ask in the background, his voice deceptively pleasant.

"Okay. I love you, Daddy," Timothy said.

"I love you, too, bud."

I was coming fucking undone.

"Thank you," Lewis said in a smug tone. "Why don't you go find the nanny? I'm sure she has some food ready by now."

I heard the patter of small footsteps, and the room went silent.

"What did I say?" Lewis asked. "He's perfectly fine. And he'll stay that way, as long as you do what I want. There's no reason this has to be anything more than a pleasant little vacation for him. Now, why don't you hand the phone back over to James?"

As he spoke, it took all my willpower not to make threats I couldn't cash over the phone. But the moment I got my hands on this fucker in person...

I reluctantly passed the phone into James's waiting hand. He was completely calm, as if this was all just a perfectly ordinary affair for him. And considering he wasn't the one whose neck was presently on the line, it was easy to see why.

What was harder to understand was what I'd been thinking when I let my guard down with him in the first place.

Now that my brothers were in the room, well aware of my faux pas—even if they didn't know it was far from a one-time deal—I was even more confused. But that all took a backseat to the pain and terror. The bittersweet gut punch of hearing Timothy's tiny voice.

For so long, I'd been afraid I was fucking this whole parenting thing up, and I was. My current situation was proof enough of that. But one fear I now knew I could lay to rest was that I didn't love him. That deep down, I was no better than Carol. Maybe even worse.

All the sleepless nights, all the isolation, all the empty, aching loneliness had felt like it was choking out everything I was supposed to feel. All the warm, fluffy feelings I'd first felt when I held him in my arms and my world narrowed down to the pinprick scope of a single person. Those feelings weren't gone, even if it was sometimes hard to see them through the fog of depression, but now...

Now, it felt like a part of me—the only part of me worth having at all—had been hollowed out. I knew it was love from the shape it had left behind, and the thought of never seeing him again left me more than empty. It wasn't even something I could fathom or dwell on for too long if I wanted to keep my sanity.

"Hello again, Lewis," James said in a calm tone that was at once infuriating and comforting. Comforting because I needed someone rational and detached to work through this, because I sure as hell wasn't either of those things. Infuriating because he had the luxury of *being* detached, and I knew better than to think there was any part of him that actually gave a damn.

Maybe he wasn't the kind of monster Lewis was, but he was still a monster nonetheless. The fact that it was easy to forget just made him all the more dangerous.

"So," James continued. "Where do we go from here?"

"Don't be so impatient," Lewis taunted. "All in good time. Just await further instruction."

I could tell he'd hung up when James looked down at the phone and quietly handed it back to me.

"That's it?" Malcolm growled. "You didn't get anything out of him."

"He got to speak to his son, didn't he?" James challenged. "We know the boy is alive, and in good condition."

"For now," Malcolm countered.

"It's a good thing he's not rushing," said James.

"How do you figure that?" Enzo demanded.

"Because it means he thinks he's still in control," James answered.

"Newsflash," I snapped. "He has my kid. He *is* in control."

"No, he isn't," James said firmly, looking me straight in the eye. "And if you start thinking that way, you can kiss your chance of ever seeing him again goodbye. This gives us time to plan."

"Time for you to plan a way to cover your ass, maybe," Malcolm said gruffly. "I still say we hand him over."

"Sure. If you want the kid to die," James said with a shrug.

"There's no reason to believe that," said Malcolm. "And every reason to believe you're lying to save your own skin, just like you always have."

"And how many successful hostage negotiations have *you* been a part of?" James asked. "Did you build your career on giving in to all the other criminals' demands, or is it just this one, because he happens to want me dead?"

Malcolm narrowed his eyes, and I could tell he was about to snap when Silas put a hand up to stop his brother. "That's enough," said Silas. "Bickering isn't going to get us anywhere, and for the night, we need to consider this a victory. If there's any benefit to Lewis, it's that he's relatively stable and he thinks he's in control. Doing anything to force his hand right now would be a mistake."

Malcolm clearly wanted to argue, but as tempted as I was to agree with him emotionally, Silas was right. We had to be rational. "So far, everything James has said has panned out," I said grudgingly. "We're not taking any risks that could set Lewis off when he has my kid."

"Forgive me if I don't trust the objective opinion of a man who's cuddled up in bed with fucking Demon," Malcolm shot back.

"You really wanna go there?" I asked through my teeth.

"Okay, enough," Silas said, pushing his brother out of the room. "No one is going anywhere tonight. Separate corners."

"This is a testosterone overload," Val muttered under his breath, taking his husband's arm. Malcolm looked like he was about to attack Silas, but one touch from Valentine was all it took to soothe the tension out of him. He wasn't going to risk hurting his beloved by fighting in such a tight space.

"Whatever," Malcolm muttered angrily, stalking off.

Valentine cast an apologetic glance over his shoulder before following him. For whatever reason, he had chosen a life of wrangling a temperamental caveman, but if that was what made him happy, who was I to judge?

I grabbed a shirt and left the room, too, because I needed some fresh air. When Silas and Enzo followed me out, closing the door behind them, I realized I had no idea what to say. There were a thousand different thoughts running through my head and that phone call had left me largely unable to parse through any of them.

"Incidentally, he has a point," said Silas.

"Yeah," said Enzo. "Care to tell me what the fuck that was about?"

"Not really," I said, folding my arms. The last thing I felt like right now was explaining myself to them. Especially when I hadn't figured out a way to explain it to myself, either.

Silas sighed. "Just be careful, Luca. James isn't someone to trifle with."

"I'm aware of that," I said. "It was a momentary lapse in judgment."

"A lapse in judgment?" Enzo scoffed. "We're talking about the Grand fucking Canyon. Since when are you even bi?"

Chapter 15

"I'm not," I snapped, pinching the bridge of my nose to fend off an impending migraine. "God, I'm not in the mood to have this conversation in the middle of the night."

"You think it's a conversation I want to be having at all?" Enzo asked. "I'm worried about you, man. Your head's understandably not on right with all this, and James is a master manipulator to put it lightly."

"I'm not being manipulated," I said stiffly. "I was pissed off, and I've been cooped up in this goddamn place with the four of you for the last week. I just needed to blow off some steam, okay? Nothing more, nothing less. And quite frankly, it's none of your fucking business."

Enzo stared at me for a few moments.

He finally sighed, looking away. "Yeah, whatever."

"Let's get some rest," Silas said, putting a hand on his husband's shoulder before looking at me. "It's probably a good idea for all of us."

I watched as they walked off down the hall, and slumped back against the wall to take a deep breath before I went back into the bedroom. I could tell they didn't buy my excuse, and it was probably just pity keeping them from pushing it, but as long as it worked, I didn't care.

If I was being honest with myself, I wasn't sure I bought the excuse, either.

I wasn't even sure I was going to have the willpower to resist if it happened again.

16

JAMES

I found myself up in the middle of the night, and not for the first time lately. It had been the better part of a week, and while Lewis hadn't called again, I'd been using the time to prepare my next move for when he did.

During the day, I had Silas breathing down my neck, which would have been far more appealing if it wasn't for his pet mafioso always being along for the ride.

That, and he cramped my research style. He had been a better boss when he gave me the free rein to do what I pleased.

Until he hadn't.

So, I was awake and combing through footage of a unicorn, A.K.A. one of the hired guns who used to work for the Capellos. He had been brought up on possession charges a couple of years back, and the archived footage was the closest I was going to get to anyone who had actually met Lewis in person.

Chapter 16

So far, the illegally obtained footage of the interrogation hadn't been particularly enlightening, and what information I had been able to glean from the footage was probably long out of date, but it was better than nothing. And I found myself thinking it was a shame that I wasn't the one handling the interrogation because the Boston PD clearly didn't have a fucking clue how to get answers out of a scumbag like him.

What else was new?

I heard movement across the room and looked up to find Luca watching me from bed, bleary-eyed. "Are you still up?" he asked, yawning.

"Your brother-in-law makes getting anything done during the day impossible with his constant hovering," I said, turning back to my screen.

Luca sat up on the edge of the bed, and I could feel him still watching me. "I don't suppose you have any breakthroughs to share?"

"Just more confirmation about what I already know," I said. "As far as I can tell, Lewis is still operating a satellite of the family business off an island somewhere in the Caribbean, with his personal headquarters still somewhere in the Northeast."

"An island?" he echoed, frowning.

"It's common for illicit operations of all varieties," I answered. "It's remote, and easy to flee by both helicopter and water transport. Find the right spot, and you don't have to worry about ending up in the wrong country's jurisdiction. Any local authorities who do catch wind are easy to pay off."

"I guess," he muttered. "You think that's where they're holding Timothy?"

"No," I answered. "For one thing, I can tell from the weather-stripping used on the windows in the photograph he sent that it was taken on the mainland."

"You what?"

"I've already been over this with Silas," I said impatiently. "Anyway, Lewis wouldn't risk exposure by taking him to his base of operations. He's probably got him at a safe house somewhere. God only knows where, but he's separate from all that, I'm quite sure," I told him.

"I guess that's a relief," Luca said, running a hand through his hair. "Sort of."

"If you'd like me to start lying and sugarcoating things to make you feel better, I can do that," I offered.

"No," Luca said quickly. "No, don't do that. I'm... I'd rather have the truth."

"Fair enough," I said. I could tell he wanted to say something else, and it was distracting. "What is it?"

"Nothing," said Luca. "Just... If I didn't know better, I'd think you actually cared about taking this guy down."

"I do," I said. "Like I said, I don't like loose ends."

"Is that really it?" he pressed, his voice laced with irritation. "Just a matter of settling an old score, or something more than that?"

Chapter 16

I sighed. "Does it matter?"

"Of course it matters," he said, his brow furrowing.

I closed the laptop and turned to face him. "You sound like your brother."

"Which one?"

"The one I don't call the dumbass," I answered. Valentine was more naive than anything, but he wasn't stupid. Granted, Enzo had somehow managed to do what I had failed to accomplish in years at Silas's side, so which of us was the fool really?

Luca rolled his eyes. "You know, you continuing to pine after Silas after all these years isn't doing any favors for your street cred."

"I wasn't aware I cared about such things," I countered. "And I'm not *pining*."

"No?" he asked. "Could've fooled me, the way you look at him."

I felt a flash of irritation. "Are you just trying to rile me up because you think it's going to lead to more hate sex? Because if you're that desperate, I can just suck you off before I get back to work. Save us both the trouble."

The irritation in his gaze suggested there might've been a grain of truth to that accusation. Amusing.

"Why do you get so defensive every time someone accuses you of being remotely human?"

"I'm not offended, I just think it's a waste of time," I said with a shrug. "So I want to bring the Capello family down. As long as you get your kid back, I don't see why my reason matters to you."

"Because my kid's life is in your hands," he said slowly. "Of course I want to know what I'm dealing with. Then there's the fact that Silas didn't break you out of prison to take the Capellos down. He broke you out to get Timothy back."

"And I'm going to do that," I assured him.

Luca stood, walking over to the table. He leaned over me, and I was pretty sure he was trying to look intimidating. Charming. Not effective, but charming.

"Look, I'm not gonna fault you for wanting to take him out," he said. "Maybe you regret some of the shit you've done, or maybe you just want to do something to make the world a little bit better to tip the scales."

"I've already made the world better," I said, blinking at him. "Why do you think I became a serial killer in the first place?"

He stared blankly back at me. He finally shook his head. "Look, after this is over and Timothy's home, I'll help you take the motherfucker out myself, but in the meantime? If you do anything to jeopardize this operation, I'll kill you."

The steel in his eyes hit differently this time. And if I were anyone else, it probably would have been intimidating.

"I respect that," I told him.

"Just so long as we have an understanding," he said, sighing as he walked back over to the bed. He paused halfway. "FYI, you can come to bed when you're ready to sleep. It's not limited to when we're... you know."

My lips pulled at the corners. I couldn't help but betray my amusement. Only a DiFiore could go from threatening a man's life to being flustered in the span of a minute.

I was beginning to see the appeal of them.

Marginally.

17

LUCA

Silas and James had been working in the kitchen for the better part of the day, and every time I checked in, it seemed like they were talking shop. At least, I didn't understand enough of it to make sense of it either way, which had me nervous.

The latest "breakthrough" was them thinking they'd figured out a way to send two-way communication through a phone line we already knew wasn't going to give us Lewis's true location.

As far as I could tell, the only thing that would possibly accomplish was pissing him off. No matter what James said, Lewis was the one calling the shots. He was the one who decided when he called, he was the one who had my son, he was the one who knew where we were while we didn't have a fucking clue where he was.

It was one fucked-up, high-stakes game of Where's Waldo with my kid's life in the hands of two men I didn't trust, even if I was considerably warier of the one than the other.

At least, I *wanted* to be.

I had every reason not to trust James, but I couldn't deny that there was still some part of me that found myself wondering—usually in the quiet moments when I lay awake and he didn't realize I was listening to him talk in his sleep about the man he was clearly still hopelessly in love with—whether he was really too far gone or not.

I wasn't sure why it mattered. It wasn't like I was in a position to save anyone. Sure as hell not him.

And I had spent the last few years chastising other members of my family for being naïve or egotistical enough to think that they had what it took to change a complete psychopath.

In short, I was a hypocrite.

A hypocrite who wasn't even gay or bi, so it should have been a moot point. There was nothing remotely logical about my attraction to James, and yet after fucking him not once but twice, not to mention thinking—and dreaming—about it more times than I cared to count, I would have to be naïve to think it wasn't there at all.

Was it even possible to have an exception like that? I had never been attracted to men before or since him, and yet, it wasn't just the spark of anger and hate chemistry that had made fucking him so memorable.

Hell, I hadn't felt anything like that in... well, ever, if I was being honest with myself.

Most days I wasn't. I had enough on my plate without opening that can of worms.

I told myself it didn't matter. Whatever this was, it was going to come to an end as soon as James was back in prison. And there was absolutely no way to avoid that outcome. He knew it as well as I did.

Hell, it wasn't like he was helping out of his own volition, no matter how dedicated he seemed. And I wasn't quite egotistical enough to believe that my threats would be enough to deter him from doing his own thing and taking Lewis out if he had the chance.

I just had to rely on him to get to the point of exchange. Then, we could figure out the rest.

I went back to "just walk by" the kitchen for what was probably the tenth time that afternoon, like anything was going to change. Silas already had it set up so that everyone would get an alert when my phone rang and it wasn't a specific set of prescreened numbers, so I knew I hadn't missed anything. Despite the fact that Silas and James were both having a highly animated conversation that had my eyes glazing over, about something overly technical, I doubted there was going to be any big breakthrough there, either.

"Kind of fucked up, isn't it?"

I turned to find Malcolm standing there watching me in the hallway, my heart racing.

"Shit, man. How does someone so big move like a fucking cat?" I muttered.

He seemed to take it as a compliment. "Just a matter of curiosity here, but look in there and tell me what you see," he said, putting a hand on my shoulder as he turned me to face the others in the kitchen.

Chapter 17

I frowned. "I don't know what you mean."

"No?" he asked. "Because it's pretty clear to me. I don't see a prisoner, do you? I see two psychos nerding out over tech shit, but I don't see a man who's wearing a collar in any meaningful sense."

I sighed. "This again..."

"Look, I don't give a shit who you stick your dick in," Malcolm said, holding his hands up. "It's none of my business, and quite frankly, I don't want to know. But I've known James long enough to know he has a way of warping reality around him. He warps *people*, and Silas is no exception."

"You think he's manipulating Silas?" I asked.

"I think anyone who thinks they can't be manipulated by James is a damn good target for him," he answered. "I think if I was you, I wouldn't want my son's life depending on a madman—or the guy who created him."

I looked back over at James, swallowing the growing lump in my throat. "You say that like we have any other options."

"I believe in making my own options," said Malcolm. "And if you want to start taking things into your own hands—instead of waiting around for that freak to call and the other freak to answer, working it all out between themselves when there's still a damn good chance they *have* been working together this whole time—you can let me know."

I narrowed my eyes. "Are you saying you have a lead on where Lewis is keeping Timothy?"

"No, but I have bait," he said, nodding to James in the kitchen. "And if you want your kid back sooner than later, I suggest we use it."

"That's a risk," I said firmly. "Even if you're right."

"I am right," he countered. "And leaving Timothy in Lewis's hands isn't a risk to you?"

I grimaced. I was starting to understand why they called Malcolm the Devil. He certainly knew how to prey on my own doubts.

"You think about it," he said, giving my shoulder a squeeze. "You know where to find me."

"Yeah," I muttered. "I'll think about it."

18

JAMES

I was in the living room for a much needed change of scenery, since Valentine was apparently out in the field putting one of the DiFiore soldiers back together after a fight, and Malcolm was sure to follow him.

I didn't want to risk running into him alone, so I mostly stayed in Luca's bedroom or in the kitchen, which was close enough to Silas's office that he would hear if Malcolm tried to attack me. Whether he would come, of course, was another matter.

I became aware of the fact that I wasn't alone and felt a twinge of apprehension, wondering if Malcolm had decided to call it a day early. When I turned around and found Luca watching me instead, I was relieved.

At least until I saw the look on his face.

He was masking it, but I could tell he was uncomfortable, which meant one of two things—he'd been talking to Malcolm, or he was getting into his own head again.

From what I had gathered of the middle DiFiore brother's nature, he was the kind of man who ruminated under normal circumstances, let alone these.

I wouldn't have been surprised if he was getting discouraged, but none of the reassurances I could offer him would assuage his emotional response.

I had to find a balance between not pissing him off by telling him something Silas and the others could confirm was a lie, and the part of me that, for some reason, didn't want to lie to him at all.

A strange revelation, if ever there was one.

"Any progress?" he asked.

"Not since we figured out how to call Lewis," I admitted. "Silas is still sorting out the details of how we can use that to our advantage."

"You think he's going to arrange the drop next time?"

"Possibly," I answered. "Or he might ask you to do something else. Just to see how much you're willing to cooperate. To test you."

"Great," he muttered.

"It won't matter if we get to him first," I said. "He knows he's vulnerable at the drop point, and he wants to make sure he's in control as much as possible before that happens."

"Seems like he's pretty fucking in control to me," said Luca.

There was no longer any doubt in my mind that he had been talking to Malcolm.

"You don't have to take my word for it," I told him. "You can ask Silas."

"I've talked to Silas," he said, his tone unreadable, but the look in his eyes said enough. "No matter how much talking we do, we're not going to see eye to eye on things. Not this."

I paused to consider his words. "I know you don't have any reason to believe me," I began. "And I would be lying if I said I didn't want to avoid a hand over for my own selfish reasons. I'm pretty sure even a DiFiore can figure that out."

Luca snorted, seemingly surprised by my response. "Thanks for the vote of confidence."

"For what it's worth, it is the best way to handle this, even if it seems counterintuitive," I continued. "You of all people should know that deals go bad all the time. When there's a hostage at stake, even more so. I know you want your son back, but I also know you're not going to do anything that would put him at more risk. He's safe right now, and I'll do whatever I can to make sure you get the chance to talk to him again. To prove that."

Luca frowned as if he wasn't expecting me to say that. Then again, he had spent enough time around Silas and Malcolm, who both saw me as some sort of comic book villain.

I couldn't really say they were wrong. Not entirely.

"Yeah," he murmured. "I would appreciate that."

There was something else in his tone now that scared me. Something so much worse than anger.

Guilt.

That wasn't good.

"I didn't come here to argue logistics, anyway," he said. "Why don't we go for a walk? I'm sure you could use some fresh air, being cooped up in here for weeks."

"A walk?" I asked doubtfully. I tapped the collar around my neck. "This doesn't come with a leash."

"Sure it does," he said, holding up the remote. "And it's not based on your proximity to the house. That would be too much of a risk if we had to get you out suddenly."

"I suppose it's a fair point," I mused. "Out of curiosity, why do you care if I have cabin fever?"

"For one thing, I'm kind of depending on you to track this asshole down," he said with a shrug. "And for another, you're still a human being. Doesn't seem right to keep you in here when you've been cooperating with everything we've asked of you so far."

"How humane," I said. And just like that, I knew he was full of shit. This was about something else, and it had Malcolm's bloody fingerprints all over it.

I stood up from the couch anyway and followed him over to the door. Luca offered me an extra coat hanging on the rack, which was just priceless.

"I suppose it's a nice opportunity to get to know each other," I mused. "Usually, I make a guy at least buy me a drink before he gets to home base."

Luca's face actually grew a bit red, and he said nothing for a moment, clearly flustered. "Yeah, whatever," he muttered, walking outside.

I couldn't help but smirk as I followed him. "Where to?"

"There's a lake not too far from here," he said, nodding at the path ahead of us.

"Quaint," I said, following him.

He was silent for most of the walk, even though I could tell from the hand in his pocket, no doubt wrapped around the remote just in case I tried to escape—or get the best of him—he was wary.

Not as wary as I was, but whatever he had planned, it wasn't like there was anything I could do about it. My entire life, I had treated the world around me like a chessboard, carefully orchestrating everything to ensure that I was the one in control.

Always in control.

Now, that simply wasn't an option, and there was something about that realization that was strangely comforting. Peaceful, at any rate. And I found myself thinking, if my fate had to be in someone else's hands, it was better that it was in Luca's than any of the other options.

19

LUCA

As I walked toward the docks, I was well aware James seemed to be able to sense something was wrong. It wasn't going to do him any good, but he hadn't said anything. He knew, though.

He was too intelligent not to. And I definitely wasn't some manipulative mastermind like Silas or Malcolm. But it didn't matter.

Malcolm had given me my task, which was to get James out of the house while Enzo and Silas were gone, and he would handle the rest. I was supposed to bring him to the docks, preferably willingly, but as we grew close enough to the water that there was no longer any room to doubt where I was taking him, it didn't matter.

Malcolm was probably already waiting in the shelter up ahead, which I could see the edge of as we drew closer.

If by some miracle James didn't know what was going on by now, he soon would, so I took the gun out of the hidden holster strapped to my chest since we were in a remote area where no one was around to see.

James looked up and didn't seem remotely surprised.

"I guess we're here," he said, looking around us as the lake water lapped at the docks. "I hope he didn't stand you up."

"How did you know?" I asked with a sigh.

He stared at me for a moment, tilting his head. "It was obvious. You were kind," he said, which was an unexpected gut punch. "There are only a few reasons why people like you are kind to people like me. It's either misguided pity, stupidity, or betrayal."

I clenched my jaw, keeping the gun trained on him. "It's not personal, James, but it's like you said. You're looking out for yourself."

"And you're looking out for your son," he said. "I get it. You're going to get him killed, but I get it."

Anger washed over me in response to his words, because even now, I knew he was just trying to get into my head. Trying to make me doubt the plan. Malcolm had warned me of it, but he didn't need to, considering it was obvious enough.

Before I could say anything, I heard the car pulling up behind us. I didn't need to be able to see in through the heavily tinted windows to know it was Malcolm.

"Right on schedule," James muttered, sounding more annoyed than angry. I wasn't sure what to make of that, but it didn't matter.

My decision was made. Now I had to live with it.

Malcolm got out of the car and walked over to us, looking right at James.

"Guess you didn't chicken out, Luca," Malcolm remarked. "Color me impressed."

"You should be ashamed of yourself," said James. "He's desperate, but *you* know better. You know this is going to get the kid killed."

Malcolm narrowed his eyes. Before I could say or do anything, he socked James in the stomach hard enough to make him double over.

"Hey!" I cried, reaching out to grab Malcolm's arm, even though he didn't seem to plan on doing anything further. "That's not what we talked about."

"What, so handing him over is fine, but roughing him up when he mouths off isn't?" Malcolm challenged.

I gritted my teeth, furious, but he had a point. "Let's just get this over with," I said, making the mistake of glancing over at James to see if he was all right. He was looking right at me, which somehow made me feel even more like shit.

"Please just cooperate," I pleaded with him, walking him over to the car where Malcolm had a fresh pair of handcuffs waiting for him.

James looked up at me when Malcolm snapped the cuffs onto his wrists. "It's not too late to call Silas and stop this."

Malcolm shoved down on his shoulder, forcing him into the car, but he wasn't being quite as rough as usual. Not that that was saying much.

Chapter 19

Fuck, what was wrong with me? Was I actually torn about this?

My kid was my first priority. He should have been my *only* priority, but there was a part of me, however irrational, that felt responsible for James. A part of me that felt protective of him, which was the biggest joke of all, because Demon of all fucking people didn't need my protection.

So why did I feel like I was betraying him? Why did his words stick in my head through the entire drive to wherever the hell it was Malcolm was taking us?

My role in the plan was over, more or less, and a part of me couldn't help but wonder if James was right. Malcolm had pushed me to act, rather than waiting on James and Silas—but was it really acting on my own if I was just going along with *his* plan instead of theirs?

I had plenty of time to contemplate it as Malcolm drove us to the outskirts of town. I recognized the mostly hidden road. And yet, I was no closer to coming to an answer as to whether I had made the right decision or not. Something told me I wasn't going to get one until Timothy was back in my arms.

James said nothing the entire time, which seemed to unsettle Malcolm as well as me. Probably because it was the one thing he couldn't scold him for.

"All right, what now?" I asked as we got out of the car and I saw Johnny and Chuck waiting for us at the docks.

"Now, we make a phone call," Malcolm said, dragging James out of the car. "Come on," he said gruffly, pushing him up the path to the main building outside the docks.

There were more armed men once we made it inside. A small army's worth of them, actually, so I knew Malcolm expected Lewis to show up. Or at least to send a proxy.

"You've got to be kidding me," James muttered, looking around at the men who were gathered at the docks. "You really think he's going to agree to this?"

"Shut up," Malcolm snapped. "I know you and Silas have a way to contact him, so do it." He unfastened the handcuffs around James's wrists. He thrust the phone into James's hands, and I could tell from the look of recognition on the other man's face that it was the one they had been working with.

"How did you get this from Silas?" James demanded.

That question seemed to irritate Malcolm, and I could tell he was about to lash out when he glanced at me and thought better of it.

"Make the call, James."

James clenched his jaw, looking over at me as if pleading for me to do something. The most unnerving thing was, I got the feeling it wasn't on his own behalf.

Was I making a mistake? There was no fucking right answer, no guide for this shit. I had to take one monster's word or another's, but no matter what my heart told me, I couldn't risk not listening to my head.

And my head said to go with the Devil I knew. Not the Demon who had an unnatural hold on me, which was probably all the more proof Malcolm was right, anyway.

Chapter 19

"Fine," James said, looking up at Malcolm. "But the kid's blood is on your hands."

The fact that he was addressing Malcolm rather than me was at once frustrating and concerning.

"Make. The. Call," Malcolm said through his teeth.

James looked down at the screen and opened some kind of program, typing in a code. I heard the phone ringing and saw James's reflection pop up on the screen. A video call.

The odds of Lewis actually answering seemed slim to none as Malcolm snatched the phone out of James's hands and waited.

To my amazement, a man I assumed was Lewis popped up on the screen. He wasn't quite what I had expected. He was clean-cut, albeit in a Mafia kind of way. He had light hair and pale blue eyes, and he didn't look a day over forty.

Not the slimy creep I had expected, but I should've known better than that. Usually, the worst monsters were beautiful. It was that much easier for them to hide in plain sight that way.

"Now this is a surprise," came Lewis's familiar voice through the speakers. "To what do I owe the pleasure?"

"Cut the crap, freak," Malcolm said, ever the diplomat. "We're done playing your game and pissing around. Now, you get to play mine. I've got something you want right here." He reached out to take James's shoulder and dragged him over to his side so he was visible on the phone's screen.

Johnny walked over to put his hands on James's shoulders and I tensed instinctively as I watched Malcolm deliver a sharp right hook to James's jaw, dropping him cold for a moment. This time, there was nothing I could do without risking Lewis thinking there was a weakness he could exploit between us.

What was done was done, and now, I had to live with the consequences.

Son of a bitch.

James staggered back to his feet, barely able to stand. Dark blood dripped from his lips.

"Something tells me you want this fucker alive," said Malcolm. "And I'm more than happy to give him to you, just like you asked. But no more fucking around. You come get him within the next hour—and don't pretend like you and your fuckers haven't been crawling all over Boston these last few nights, because we both know that's bullshit—or there might not be anything left for you to collect. Choice is yours."

"And here I thought I was dealing with competent men," Lewis said, his voice dripping with condescension and annoyance more than genuine anger.

"An hour, Capello," Malcolm reiterated. "Something tells me you know exactly where to find us, but I made it easy. Check the phone and do whatever you have to do to get here. Or don't. More fun for me that way."

As soon as he hung up, I lunged, shoving Malcolm in the chest as hard as I could. He actually staggered back, which was a surprise.

"Are you out of your fucking mind?" I spat. "That wasn't the plan!"

Chapter 19

"My game, my rules," Malcolm said, shoving me back. "You're welcome, by the way. You can wait to thank me until he gets here."

Before I could respond, the sound of laughter interrupted us. I looked over to find James, who had collapsed against the railing along the top of the wall, slumped over with his shoulders shaking in what seemed to be genuine laughter.

"You fucking fool," he said, shaking his head.

Malcolm struck him hard enough that I could tell James had gotten the air knocked out of him, and Malcolm was going in for another hit when I grabbed him by the shoulder, dragging him back.

"I said that's enough," I snarled, well aware the others were watching us.

Chuck and Johnny especially. They didn't know what to do now that two of their leaders were fighting. As the second oldest in the family, and a direct descendent of our former Don, my authority took precedence over Valentine's husband's, at least in theory.

I knew better than to think it would always work out like that in practice, though, even if I had known them all our lives, and Malcolm was still technically an outsider.

Before we could figure out which way the wind would blow, I heard the sound of an engine in the distance. A boat?

No, a fucking helicopter.

"Shit," Chuck muttered, pulling his gun out of the holster on his hip. "They were close."

"That's the idea, dipshit," Malcolm said, clearly not open to any criticism of the plan.

What else was new?

There was a boat cutting through the water up ahead at a blazing speed, so I got my own gun ready and reached to pull James to his feet.

"Get him into the shelter," Malcolm ordered, even though I was already on my way.

Once we were inside the building next to the docks, I pushed James behind the wall in the middle line of shelving that would at least provide some cover for us before finding a gap in the wooden planks boarding up a window that I could look through.

I could see the water itself, but there was no gunfire yet, which was a good sign. Probably.

"Call Silas," James said, looking up at me.

There was already a bruise forming along his jaw where Malcolm had hit him. The sight made my stomach churn for various reasons, but I had to push all that aside for the moment. If I didn't keep my head, none of us were getting out of this alive.

"Shut up," I muttered under my breath, even as I wondered if he was right.

I strained to get a better look at the figure standing on the end of the boat. At first, I thought it might be Lewis, but I realized it was just someone who looked vaguely like him. Then I saw him raise his rifle and the gunfire began from all sides.

"Shit," I muttered, grabbing James to force his head down. Once he was covered, I fired through the slats in the window and ducked again. I covered my ears as the harsh whipping sound of the helicopter's blades grew closer and the shack trembled around us.

"Yes, excellent job," said James. "This is really an ingenious plan."

"Would you shut up?" I growled, firing at another one of Lewis's men. I got in a shot, but there was no way to tell if it was fatal before I was forced to take cover again.

"If you want to live, uncuff me and give me the gun. You're a terrible shot," James said pointedly.

I glared at him over my shoulder. "I'm not giving you the fucking gun," I said through my teeth, but I hastily uncuffed him.

I fired again, and the last glimpse I got out the window, I had been able to see at least Johnny and Malcolm were still alive.

Malcolm was right about one thing—Lewis hadn't had time to assemble an army. We'd caught him off guard, and he was desperate enough to come and try to catch the bait.

Just not desperate enough to show up himself.

I was taking aim at another one of the men who had gotten off the boat when I felt a slight movement at my side and turned around to find that James had grabbed the other gun out of the holster beneath my jacket while I was distracted. He raised it and took aim, and I froze, filled with a myriad of conflicting emotions.

Fear. Anger. Regret.

And, most absurd of all, betrayal.

James shifted the gun to fire just over my head, and I spun around in time to see a man I hadn't even realized had crept into the building hit the ground.

James lowered the gun slightly, his eyes taking on a familiar coldness. As I stood there, staring like a fucking idiot, I couldn't even bring myself to do anything.

"You're welcome," he muttered before darting past me and slipping out the door the way the other man had come.

"Hey!" I cried, rushing after him. "Wait!"

Before I could follow him, there was an impact of something striking the outside of the shack, and the next thing I knew, I was flying across the room, red and yellow flashes of light blinding me.

My head hit the ground and I blacked out.

When I came to—something I really didn't expect to happen at all—my ears were ringing, and there were still flashes of light in my eyes. I managed to get up on my hands and knees, then onto my feet, staggering through the rubble of the building.

There was a disembodied arm draped atop an empty box and another body across the room, and I had no idea who either belonged to.

I stumbled outside. The smoke was choking my lungs, and I couldn't stop coughing. I still had my gun, somehow, even though I couldn't remember grabbing it again.

Outside, the air really wasn't much better. I could hardly see through the smoke, but I heard Chuck's voice somewhere

Chapter 19

and caught a glimpse of Johnny, lying unconscious on the edge of the docks. Before I could go over to him, I heard the click of a gun and spun around to find a man I didn't recognize staring me down, taking aim at my forehead.

"Where is he?" he demanded. "Demon."

I reluctantly held my hands up, my finger on the side of the gun rather than the trigger. I knew the answer to that question was the only thing keeping me alive at the moment, as I was still struggling to think.

"You tell me where your boss is, and I'll tell you where he is," I countered.

The man's lips curved into a smirk. "You're not really in any position to be bargaining right now, are you?" he challenged.

He had a point, of course.

Before I could respond, I heard the sound of an engine in the distance and tires tearing up the dirt. When a sleek black sports car barreled into the man in front of me, killing him on impact, my body froze in shock.

As the car swerved to a stop and the door to the passenger side opened, I reached for my gun, ready to defend myself until I saw who was in the driver's seat.

"James?"

20

LUCA

"Get in," James ordered, pushing the door open from across the car. Blood was soaking through the front of his shirt on his right side, and there was more of it on his face, although it was hard to say whose it was.

Why he wasn't adding mine to the palette was a mystery my shell-shocked brain was too jumbled to piece together. Why he was saving me was even more of one.

I leaped into the passenger's seat and slammed the door behind me as the rear window exploded in another peal of gunfire.

"Shit," I hissed, ducking down to cover my head.

James peeled out of the docks like it was no big deal. Just another Friday for him. Then again, he was a serial killer and Silas's former apprentice, so it probably was.

"Stop being such a pussy," he muttered. "You're acting like it's the first time you've ever been shot at."

Chapter 20

"It's not the first," I snapped. "It's just not a regular occurrence."

"You have your gun?"

I checked beneath my jacket just to make sure it was still there. "Yeah, why?"

"Coming up on our left," he answered, taking a sharp turn that tossed me against the door. "Aim for the tires, and for fuck's sake, put on your goddamn seat belt."

"Right," I muttered, turning around. I fired through the broken rear windshield a few times before I hit the front right tire, and the car went spinning out, hitting the side of the nearest building.

I got back in my seat and buckled up.

"Look at that," James said dryly. "You would almost think you were a Mafia man."

I glared at him, but considering he had just saved my life, I couldn't really be too pissed. Which raised a pertinent question.

"Why the fuck did you do that?" I asked. "You could've gotten away."

"It had crossed my mind," he said, keeping his eyes on the road. He sounded vaguely annoyed, but I wasn't sure if it was with himself or me. "Maybe I just wanted to save you for myself."

Coming from him, those words should have been chilling. Unfortunately, they weren't.

"Well, whatever your reason was... thank you."

"Don't thank me yet," he said, glancing in the rearview mirror. "We'll be lucky to get out of this alive, and thanks to your brother-in-law, negotiations just got reset to zero."

"Yeah, I'm aware," I said bitterly. I had plenty to blame on myself, too. "Should have known Lewis wouldn't be there."

"You should have," James agreed. "I seem to recall telling you. And yet, you chose to believe Malcolm."

"I know," I said through my teeth. "I'm sorry, okay? I fucked up. I get it, and I know I don't have the right to ask this of you, or even have any leverage at this point, but please... help me get Timothy back. I'll do whatever it takes, just please, don't give up."

"Would you stop begging?" he muttered, grimacing. "If there's one thing I can't stand, it's desperation."

"You'll do it, then?" I asked hopefully.

He narrowed his eyes, glancing over at me for a second before focusing back on the road. "If I help you, it's not for you," he said. "It's because it *happens* to align with my unfinished business with the Capello family, and because there's an innocent child involved who doesn't deserve to die just because his father and uncle are fucking idiots."

"Fair enough," I said.

"And there are conditions," he added.

I sighed. Of course there were. "What do you want?"

"You will do as I say," he said firmly. "No exceptions. No second-guessing. No questions."

I was surprised that was all he wanted. "Okay. I can agree to that."

He said nothing for a few minutes, and when he finally spoke, his voice was low. "We can't involve the others. As you've seen for yourself, Malcolm's judgment can't be trusted, and Silas clearly can't control him."

"Yeah," I said. "No argument there."

"We're on our own," James added pointedly. "That's the way it has to be. If you don't like it, I'll pull over right now and you can walk home or wherever the hell else you want, but if you get any ideas while we're out there or even think about doublecrossing me again, I'll fucking kill you. And when I save your kid, I'm going to tell him his father was a fucking idiot. Do we have an understanding?"

I stared at him for a moment before sighing. "Yeah," I finally answered. "We do."

That seemed to satisfy him, at least. He flinched suddenly, so I looked to see if there was anything else on the road with us, but there wasn't.

"You all right?" I asked warily.

"I'm fine," he said through his teeth.

"You don't look fine," I told him, eyeing his side. "How many times did you get shot?"

"Once," he answered. "Maybe twice."

"Maybe?" I echoed in dismay. "You don't know how many times you got shot?"

"Who keeps track of that kind of thing?" he asked. "It's tedious. Either way, I'll be fine."

"Will you?" I asked doubtfully. I was hit, too, but the bullet had only grazed my arm, and aside from a few ribs that felt busted, there wasn't much lasting damage as far as I could tell. "Because right now, it looks like you're about to bleed out on the side of the road."

"If I stop now, they'll find us," he said.

I wasn't sure if he meant Lewis's men or Malcolm's, but either way, he had a point.

"At least let me drive."

I could tell he wanted to argue, but he finally pulled over to switch sides. His gait was uneven as he walked past me across the dirt road and got in on the other side, but I figured if he was still capable of standing on two feet, that was probably a good sign.

The moment we got back onto the road, James slumped against his seat. He took off his belt and his shirt, rumpled it up to push it against the worst of his wounds, then wrapped his belt around his upper waist as tightly as he could before locking it in place.

It wasn't ideal, but I guess it was good enough for the moment.

"Where am I going?" I asked.

"Just get onto the highway, and take the second exit you see," he answered. "We're making a quick stop."

"A stop?" I asked.

Before I could say anything else, he shot me a venomous look. "What did I say about questions?"

"Right," I muttered. "Almost forgot."

I drove faster, because no matter what he said, he definitely wasn't fine. There was only so much a body could take in his condition, and I found myself worried for more than just my own sake.

Eventually, the exit came up, to my infinite relief.

"Where now?" I asked.

"There's a warehouse about half a mile from here," he answered. "I'll tell you when to take the turn."

As tempted as I was to ask why the fuck we were going to a warehouse, I didn't. Sure enough, we ended up in some industrial district. I turned onto the small dirt road when he pointed out the correct building.

"Park by the water," he ordered.

I hadn't even noticed the lake up ahead beyond the building, separating it from the other warehouses in the district, but I complied.

James reached over the center console and put the car into neutral after I parked. He got out and went around behind it, and I quickly followed him once I realized what he was doing.

"Hey, you can't push that," I snapped.

He stepped back, gesturing for me to do it. "Go ahead then, muscleman."

I sighed. Getting rid of the car probably wasn't a bad idea, but even if it had a black box to track us with, we had more pressing issues.

"There's a tracker inside you," I pointed out.

"Which is why we're here. Now hurry up and ditch the car."

He didn't bother to elaborate, so I kept my mouth shut and pushed the car into the lake. It sank as I followed him into the building, finding myself wondering if I was walking into a trap. Not that he needed to lay one. He could've left my ass for dead without lifting a finger if getting rid of me was what he really wanted, and I wouldn't even have blamed him.

The warehouse was mostly empty, but there were white sheets covering what I assumed was abandoned machinery. The place looked like it had been a textile factory or something at one point, and there was no shortage of old mills in the region, most of them located by the water for the runoff. This area just wasn't swanky enough for most of them to have been converted into overpriced lofts.

The walls were made of thick heavy metal, and while I had ditched my phone a long time ago, I seriously doubted I would've gotten a signal anyway.

"It's a dead zone," James said, as if reading my thoughts.

"Will that keep them from tracking the chip?" I asked.

"Not forever, but it'll certainly help," he replied, walking toward a set of flimsy metal stairs that led up into the overhead loft. I followed him, watching as he went over to investigate one of the floorboards where a chunk was missing. He stuck his hand into the chipped board and gave it a sharp tug, wincing as the whole plank came up.

Chapter 20

I watched as he pulled out a black duffel bag and started gathering the things from inside it, along with something that looked a lot like Val's field kit.

"This is your safe house?" I asked doubtfully.

"One of them," he said. "And it's only going to be useful for another fifteen, maybe twenty minutes tops, so get over here and make yourself useful."

"Field medicine really isn't in my repertoire," I admitted, even though it probably should have been after all the shit that had gone down over the last couple of years.

"Just do what I tell you and it'll be fine. Probably," he said, taking out a scalpel from the rolled set in the kit. He handed it to me and sat down on the floor with his legs crossed, sweeping his hair away from his neck. "You need to remove my implant."

I stared at the scalpel, then at him. "Shouldn't we be more worried about the bullets?"

"Malcolm is probably trying to track us as we speak," he said pointedly. "Assuming Silas isn't trying to kill him for fucking with the plan. I'm counting on that to buy us another couple of minutes, actually. And what did I say about questions?"

"Right," I mumbled, sitting down next to him. I put my left hand on his shoulder and hesitated. "Where is it at? How do I get it out without setting off the collar?"

"Carefully," James replied. He reached behind his back and felt around along his upper shoulders, his fingers circling around a spot just below the collar. "Feel that?"

I touched the spot where his hand was, running my fingers over his skin until I could feel the raised object beneath his flesh. "Yeah, I feel it."

"Good. Cut about a half-inch deep just below it and it'll pop right out," he told me.

"It's going to hurt," I said, at the risk of stating the complete obvious. "You want something to bite down on, or—?"

"Just do it or I'll do it myself," he ordered.

I clenched my jaw, trying to get over the revulsion that he clearly didn't share. I sliced into his flesh, a bit too shallow at first, and before he could snap at me, I went deeper, opening up a gash that was about half an inch deep and three quarters of an inch wide. Blood trickled from the wound, running down his back in rivulets.

"That's good," he said. "Now apply pressure on either side of the cut."

"I take it you've done this before," I mumbled, doing as he said.

"Plenty of times. Silas likes to have backups," he said.

I grimaced as a chip popped out of the wound, about the size of two grains of rice. I dropped the bloodied chip onto the floor and used my sleeve to apply pressure to the wound.

James didn't so much as make a sound, even if his breath did hitch slightly. He was already focused on the wound on his side, and my stomach churned as I watched him digging into the open hole in his flesh with a pair of forceps.

"Can I just—"

Chapter 20

Before I could even finish that thought, something that sounded like metal clinked against the floor and he breathed an audible sigh of relief. "Got it in one piece."

"Lucky, I guess," I said, cringing as I studied the bloody bullet on the floor. I watched as he stitched himself up over the next few minutes before discarding the used implements and rolling the rest of them back up into the set. He placed that back into the bag and zipped it all up.

I grabbed the bag from him before he could put it over his shoulder.

"I know you're like an unfeeling cyborg or whatever, but at least try to take it easy," I pleaded.

He rolled his eyes and started back down the stairs. I followed him over to one of the large, covered objects across the room and he nodded to it. "Since you're in a chivalrous mood, pull that off."

I grabbed the edge of the fabric tarp and tore it off, revealing the shiny gray-and-black motorcycle beneath it.

"You really keep this place stocked, don't you?" I asked.

"There are clothes behind that machine," he said, nodding up ahead.

Sure enough, there was another duffel bag full of them. They were close enough to my size, so I changed into a fresh pair of jeans and a black shirt that wasn't covered in blood before handing a fresh change of clothes to James, along with my old shirt so he could clean himself up a little.

"Do you know how to drive one of these?" he asked, getting something out of the compartment on the back of the bike. He tossed me a set of keys.

"Of course I know how to drive a bike," I said, climbing on and starting the engine. "This is going to be rough on you, though."

"Probably," he agreed, climbing onto the bike behind me. "Try not to hit any potholes."

"This is New England. The whole state is one giant pothole punctuated by brief patches of cement."

He grunted in acknowledgment and I waited until he wrapped his arms tightly around me from behind to start off. I pulled out of the lot behind the warehouse, trying to avoid any major pits in the dirt road, which was easier said than done.

"Get on the interstate," he told me. "Drive until you can't anymore. Or until I pass out. Then we'll find somewhere to stay the night and regroup."

"That's really reassuring," I said dryly.

The fact that I had just watched a man treat his own gunshot wound in a fucking warehouse and wasn't insisting on going to the hospital—and that wasn't even a remote possibility—was just proof of what a sharp left-hand turn my life had taken lately.

James was silent for hours as I drove, and every now and then, I would have to call his name to bring him back to me. When I felt his grip weakening around my waist, I knew it was time.

Chapter 20

I found a motel in a small, inconsequential town I had chosen to stop in. To my relief, the clerk behind the front desk was so intently focused on the porn on his computer screen that he barely gave me a second glance before taking my money and handing me the room key.

James had agreed to wait outside, since the fewer people who saw our faces, the better. I went out to meet him and led him to our room on the second floor, which he had insisted on. When I saw how unsteady he was on his feet, I draped his arm over my shoulder to help him.

The fact that he didn't complain about that probably wasn't a great sign for how he was doing.

"You okay?" I asked, even though that was probably a pretty dumb question.

The fact that he didn't call me on it *definitely* wasn't a good sign.

"I'm fine," he said, his voice strained.

I opened the motel room door, trying not to think about how sick I felt.

There was so much I hadn't even had time to process since it had all gone down. There was the fear for my son that never left or even waned, not for an instant. And now, there was fear for this man I barely knew alongside it. All I really did know of him was that he was a criminal mastermind who had an insane body count.

A criminal mastermind who had saved my life. One I had to rely on if I ever wanted to see my son alive again.

I helped James into the bed and he immediately collapsed on his side.

"I'll get you something to drink," I said, looking around until I found a shitty coffee maker on the dresser with a few plastic cups next to it. I grabbed one and went into the bathroom to pour some water I was honestly shocked didn't come out brown, considering the general state of this place.

Not that an abandoned warehouse was a much more sterile environment.

"Here," I said, holding the cup to James's lips since he didn't look capable of drinking on his own. To my surprise, he actually let me help him drink and drained the cup.

"How is your wound?" I asked, looking down at the fresh stitches in his side as I lifted his shirt. That was going to leave one hell of a scar.

"I'll be fine," he said dismissively. "Didn't hit any organs."

"Is there anything I can get you?" I asked. I hated feeling useless, and that was something I'd had to swallow a lot of lately.

"There are pills in that bag," he said, nodding toward the duffel bag.

"Sure," I said, walking over to unzip the bag and rummage through his medical kit. "Uh. There's a small pharmacy in here. Which ones do you need?"

"Amoxicillin and oxycodone," he answered. "Two of each."

I searched through the bottles until I found the right ones, shook out the pills, and went over to offer them to him along with a fresh cup of water.

Chapter 20

"You lost a lot of blood," I said as he swallowed them down. "I know you don't trust the others, but maybe Valentine—"

"No," he said through his teeth. "I told you, I'm fine. I just need to rest."

"Okay," I said, holding my hands up. "I'll watch the door."

He said nothing as he lay back on his side, closing his eyes.

I got up to turn out the lights and moved the curtain to peek out the window, even though I couldn't see anything on the quiet street below.

By the time I turned back, James was out cold. If it wasn't for the steady rise and fall of his chest, which I found myself fixating on intently for the next few hours, I wouldn't have been able to tell he was alive.

I sank into the chair next to the bed and set my gun on the table next to me. I leaned forward, burying my face in my hands and raking my fingers through my hair.

What a fucking day.

21

JAMES

I opened my eyes and was pleasantly surprised to find I was still alive. I was equally surprised that Luca was still awake, despite looking plenty exhausted in his own right.

"What time is it?" I asked, rubbing my eyes. Of course this place didn't even have a bedside clock.

It seemed my former captor had the same taste in motels as he had in life partners. Cheap, trashy, and entirely temporary.

"A little after three in the morning," he answered. "How are you feeling?"

"Like shit," I answered, sitting up. The room spun, but it stopped, so there was that.

"You kind of look like shit, so that checks out."

I snorted, getting up from the bed. Luca leaped up from his chair, grabbing me by the shoulders to steady me, which was just as well, considering the fact that my legs started to give out the second my feet hit the floor.

"Easy," he muttered, helping me back onto the edge of the bed. "You're not going anywhere for a while."

"We can't stay here," I told him.

"You sure as hell can't get back on that bike," I said. "At least let me go out and find something more reliable."

"More reliable?" I asked flatly. "What are you going to do, rent a car with your credit card?"

"Of course not," he muttered, rubbing the back of his head.

I rolled my eyes. "Have you ever even stolen anything in your life?"

"Yes, I've stolen shit." He sounded grievously offended.

"Oh, really?" I challenged. "Let me guess, the nice neighbor had a sign saying to take one piece of candy on Halloween, and you took three?"

"I'm not Valentine," he scoffed. "My friend Geo and I stole his father's car when we were fifteen. And I stole Johnny's girlfriend once, if that counts."

I shook my head. "You really are the Waltons of the Mafia."

"Says the man who watches that show."

"Fine. Today's your lucky day," I said. "Today's the day I teach you how to steal a car. One that doesn't belong to your daddy's best friend."

He shrugged. "If you're up for it. I'll go check out.

I stared blankly at him for long enough that he mumbled, "Right. Never mind. Let's just go."

Once we were outside, I looked around the lot, not thrilled with the options. "I'll be fine on the bike for a short distance. I'm assuming you're going to have another bout of guilty conscience if we steal a car from someone who needs it."

Luca hesitated. "I guess I would prefer if this was more of a Robin Hood thing."

"Good God," I said under my breath, walking over to the bike and climbing on, sitting back to make room for the saint.

About ten minutes later, we were in a parking lot in the back of an apartment complex. It was filled with a decent number of cars that didn't look like they were going to break down after a few hours on the highway.

I took a black leather roll out of my jacket and pulled out the slim jim tucked inside one of the pouches for just such an occasion. I slid the thin metal rod in between the door and the frame, and it opened easily enough, but when I started to get in, Luca blocked me.

"I got it," he said, slipping into the driver's seat. He popped open the console and started hotwiring the car with unexpected ease.

"Color me impressed," I said, climbing into the passenger's side seat.

"So, where to?" Luca asked.

"My safe house," I answered. "We need to regroup and find a way to get back in contact with Lewis as quickly as possible.

While hiding from your brothers and their pet psychopaths, obviously."

"How are we supposed to do that?" he asked. "Something tells me you don't have Lewis's number on speed dial."

"No, but I can port your number and intercept your calls once I have my equipment," I said.

"And you're sure Silas doesn't know about the safe house?"

"If he did, he would've killed me a long time ago."

"Great." Luca grew silent for a few minutes, which was fine with me. I wasn't really in a chatting mood.

I was trying not to take the betrayal personally, considering the fact that I was a practical stranger, and his kid's life was on the line. That didn't mean I wasn't pissed.

"Can I ask you a personal question?"

"Sure, why not?" I shrugged. "It's not like this is a road trip from hell or anything."

"What do you see in him?" he asked. "Silas, I mean."

I looked over at him, raising an eyebrow. That was an unnecessary clarification, if ever there was one. "You really need to ask me that when your brother is married to him?"

"Hey, I don't get that, either," he said, lifting his fingers off the wheel. "But Enzo is a simple guy. You're not. I guess I just don't see what's so appealing about a megalomaniacal sociopath who treats all but the partial handful of people he cares about like pawns in a chess game."

"Birds of a feather, I suppose."

"That's bullshit," he said, to my surprise. "Yeah, I admit, you and Silas seem similar enough on the surface, but you're not. You're not like him, or Malcolm. My brothers may have brought out some other side of them, but they're still both... empty. Cold."

"You said it yourself," I said in a flat tone. "I'm a serial killer."

"Yeah, but you killed perverts and monsters," Luca countered. "And something tells me you didn't just wake up one day and decide you were going to start a brand-new career hacking people up without reason."

"Don't romanticize me, Luca," I said, looking out the window. "I'm not some misunderstood vigilante."

"Maybe not," he conceded. "But you're not the cold-blooded, remorseless killer you want everyone to think you are, either. At least, that's not *all* you are."

I fell silent, because I wasn't sure I liked the direction this conversation was headed. Or how to respond to it. "What do you want, Luca?"

"What do you mean?" he asked.

"What are you trying to get out of this?" I clarified. "Is it the cognitive dissonance? You've been shitting on your brothers for falling for psychopaths for so long that you can't handle the fact that you might be a hypocrite? Because if it's that, I can reassure you right now that you don't actually care about me. You're not even interested in me."

He looked over at me, frowning. "And what makes you so sure of that?"

I wasn't expecting that to be his response, either. "Because it's true," I replied. "You're not gay. You're not even bisexual. You're just emotionally vulnerable, and I excel at manipulating people."

"Manipulating?" he echoed. "So that's what that was? You were just manipulating me into fucking you? Why would you even bother to do that?"

I shrugged. "Maybe I was bored. And maybe it seemed like something that could work in my favor, eventually. There would've been a chance to escape, sooner or later."

Luca clenched his jaw and started driving a little faster, even though I was sure he didn't realize it. "That's bullshit, too."

"Whatever you need to tell yourself."

"Back at you," he countered. "Because I think you're the one who's struggling with a little 'cognitive dissonance.'"

"And how do you figure that?" I asked with a bored sigh.

"Because you made a mistake," he replied. "I think you slipped up and let yourself be a little too vulnerable. I think you let yourself be human, even just for a moment, with someone who betrayed you, and you're the one who can't handle that."

I gave a dry laugh that sounded more bitter than I wanted to admit. "Is that what happened?" I taunted. "My, you think highly of yourself."

"Am I wrong?" he challenged.

"You are, as a matter of fact," I said. "But it doesn't really matter."

"I guess I'm wrong about why you love Silas, too," he said. "Because I was starting to have a theory on that."

"You're starting to bore me."

"I think you love him because he's the first person who made you feel needed," he continued, ignoring me. "The first person who made you feel like you mattered, even if it was only because he wanted to use you."

"Shut up," I hissed, my voice coming out more venomous than I intended. "You don't know what you're talking about."

"Don't I?" he challenged. "Because I'm pretty sure that's why you're so pissed off. And maybe you're right. Maybe you are good at manipulating people. But I've known Silas for long enough to know that he's better at it. And I'm not saying any of this to shit on you, because I know what that's like. I know what it's like to think you meant something to someone, only to find out they were just using you. So trust me. I get it."

"You don't get anything," I replied. "You think you know how I feel because your childhood sweetheart dumped you? Because your daddy was mean? You don't have any idea who I am, or what I've been through, and you sure as hell don't know what I feel."

Luca was silent for a few moments, his knuckles turning white on the wheel. "Maybe not," he finally said, his voice quieter. "But I know what it's like to feel like no one understands you. I know what it's like to be alone, and I'm just trying to say... you don't have to be. Not if you don't want to."

I laughed. "Luca DiFiore is going to save me from myself. How quaint."

"I never said that," he said. "And I'm not... saying I'm gay or bi or whatever. Or that I would be ready for a relationship, even if I was. But no matter what you think, I *do* care about you. And I'm sorry for what happened. I'm sorry for handing you over to Malcolm. It was a mistake on a shit ton of levels."

"Are you still on about that?" I asked. "God, it must be exhausting holding onto shit all the time. Feeling guilt."

"Look, I'm apologizing, okay?" he asked. "You can take it or leave it."

"Whatever." I sighed. "It's water under the bridge. People do stupid things for love."

I knew that better than anyone.

"Yeah," he said quietly. "I guess they do."

We didn't talk for the rest of the drive, which was ideal for me. I didn't need any more of Luca's driver's seat psychiatry.

The fact that his words were still crawling under my skin all this time later, however, gave me reason to wonder if he was right. At least about some of it.

22

LUCA

We drove for what felt like an eternity before we finally came to James's safe house in the mountains. He seemed to be doing better, at least. He was as stalwart physically as he was mentally, despite not really looking like the sturdiest person.

"So," I said, as I carried his duffel bag into the small but comfortable cabin. "Since you didn't blindfold me on the way here, does that mean you trust me? Or that you're planning on killing me?"

"Neither," he answered, heading straight for the fireplace across the room. It was pretty cold, so I assumed he was going to throw a log on or something, but instead, he flipped some kind of latch behind the mantelpiece and the entire thing slid open, revealing a secret passageway behind the fireplace.

Of course.

"It means the safe house is going to be useless after this," he continued.

Chapter 22

Oh. I wasn't expecting that.

"Holy shit," I muttered. "Is this your underground lair or something?"

"One of them," he said without a hint of irony, disappearing into the darkness.

"Hey, wait," I called, dropping the duffel bag to follow him.

He flipped another switch on the wall. The LED lights stretched across the top of the stone ceiling came on one after the other, lighting up a long hallway that seemed to stretch on forever.

"Damn," I muttered, looking around the underground facilities. There were computers everywhere and a bunch of monitors set up all along one wall. There was a small laboratory set up in one corner of the space, and while it looked like it hadn't been used in some time, I didn't even want to know what that was for. "This looks like Silas's man cave."

"The one *you* know about," he scoffed.

Okay, now I was going to be paranoid when I got back home. Not that that was anything new.

"This is quite the setup," I said. "You have everything you need here?"

"Yes," he said, sitting down in front of one of the computers and turning it on. The screens all came to life immediately. The whole place seemed to be running on a separate generator that must've activated when we had come downstairs. State of the art. But that was really no surprise, considering who James was.

I hung back, feeling like a useless slob while he got to work. "Right," I said, running a hand through my hair. "I guess I'll just... go upstairs and see if I can find something for us to eat."

"Mhm," James said absently, still fixated on the screen.

I had a feeling I wouldn't be missed as I poked around the building to get a lay of the land. The kitchen seemed surprisingly well stocked, even though everything was canned or otherwise shelf stable. It was a prepper's paradise, including the glorified nuclear bunker in the basement.

When I came back downstairs a couple of hours later, not wanting to distract James from doing his thing but also unable to keep my nervous curiosity at bay for too long, he was right where I'd left him.

"Any progress?" I asked.

"Plenty," he answered, taking out a phone that looked like it was from the '90s. This place had everything. Probably shit I didn't even want to know about. "I ported your number through to all my devices. Now, we just have to wait for him to contact us."

"Yeah," I said. "I guess that's all there is to do."

"He won't hurt your kid," James said after a few moments. "What Malcolm did was reckless, and that set us back, but Lewis won't give up that easily. He knows Timothy is his only bargaining chip, and the only thing that's keeping Silas from destroying the mountains he's trying to pick apart piece by piece right now. He knows Silas is avoiding causing an avalanche that won't matter at all if Lewis kills your son."

Chapter 22

I swallowed hard. Comfort definitely wasn't in this guy's wheelhouse, but his words were reassuring in a strange way, all the more so because of their bluntness. He wasn't trying to assuage a nervous father's feelings, he was simply telling the truth, and that gave me something I needed desperately.

It gave me hope.

And in the absence of being able to do anything else, the other thing I sorely needed was a distraction.

"Come on," I said, nodding my head in the direction of the stairs. "It's about time you ate something. You lost a lot of blood, and you need to replenish."

"Are you my doctor now?"

"Why not?" I asked. "Between the two of us, we have the same number of medical degrees."

"Touché," he said dryly, following me up the stairs. Halfway up, he suddenly winced and doubled over, gripping his side.

"James?" I cried, reaching for him.

"I'm fine," he said through his teeth. "Just my stitches."

"I can carry you," I offered. He gave me a withering look, so I added, "Or I could just help you up the stairs."

He grudgingly draped an arm over my shoulder and shifted more of his weight onto me as we headed back up the stairs.

"There. Nice and easy," I said.

"Don't," he warned.

"Don't what?"

"Don't be annoyingly nice to me just because you feel like shit."

"What makes you think I feel like shit?" I asked.

He gave me a look. "Please. You're the second son of an Italian Catholic family who recently fucked another guy. You're a cluster of self-doubt, shame, and daddy issues in a trenchcoat."

I grunted. "Be that as it may, I'm trying to help."

"I don't need your help. And I certainly don't need your pity."

"I never said I pitied you."

"You didn't need to. It's on the neon sign scrolling across your eyes."

I sighed, helping him into a chair at the kitchen table before sitting across from him. "Most of the cans were expired, so it's spaghetti and lima beans for dinner. I'll try to find other stuff in the morning."

"Don't bother. I'll have someone do the shopping while we're here," he said, taking a bite of the pasta. He paused, stared at it for a second, then kept eating, which I took as proof I was as shitty of a cook as I had always feared.

"Isn't that a risk?" I asked. When he continued to stare at me, I said, "No questions... right. Sorry."

We continued to eat in silence, and I cleared the dishes once we were both finished. "You can take the room upstairs," James said as I finished cleaning. He stretched like a cat as he got up from the table. "I've got an alarm set to go off throughout the cabin if the phone rings, so there's no need to worry about missing the call."

"Oh," I said, since that addressed my knee-jerk reaction to his plan to separate for the night. But it didn't change my opinion. If anything, I was as reluctant about the idea as I had been before. "I'm just not sure it's a good idea to separate, you know? Not with you being this fucked up. What if something happens and you go downhill during the night?"

"What are you going to do about it if I do?" he asked.

"I mean, I could call an ambulance," I said.

He scoffed. "You really think that's a good idea? I'm sure Malcolm has every badge in the country looking for me at this point."

"It's a better idea than letting you bleed to death," I told him. "And even if I can't do anything, I still don't like the idea of leaving you alone, okay?"

I expected him to argue, and considering how he was just staring blankly at me, I was sure he was going to. Instead, he just shrugged and walked down the hall. "Fine. Do what you want."

Well, that was better than nothing.

As I followed him into the room, I was pleasantly surprised by its warm and inviting atmosphere. The handmade quilts that were draped over the bed, set within a rustic log frame, added a cozy touch to the space. The chandelier made of antlers casting a soft glow from the ceiling was a unique touch. That must have been why there were spiny shadows all over the walls.

"Nice decor," I said, walking into the room. Judging from the ice in his eyes as he looked over his shoulder, he thought I was fucking with him. "I wasn't being sarcastic."

"Then I'm even more insulted," he said, reaching to pull off his shirt.

"Here, let me help you with that," I said, helping him get it over his head the rest of the way so he didn't have to lift his arms up.

To my relief, he didn't fight me. Of course, that might just have been because he was too tired to fight, but still.

"That looks like it hurts," I said, looking down at the wound on his side.

"It's fine," he muttered, brushing his fingers over the bruised area beneath the stitches. "It'll heal. But I should get cleaned up more thoroughly."

"Yeah," I said, walking over to open the door to what I assumed was the bathroom. I turned on the light and realized it was bigger than I had expected. There was a clawfoot tub on the far side of the room, so I went over to fill it.

Out of the corner of my eye, I could see James getting undressed the rest of the way and resisted the urge to look for some reason.

"Come on," I said, offering a hand. "I'll help you in."

James's eyes narrowed and he walked past me, stepping into the bathtub. Try as I might to avoid it, my eyes kept drifting to travel over his body.

"Are you just going to stand there watching me? Or are you coming in?" he asked in his usual bone-dry tone.

I blinked. I hadn't planned on it, but the invitation was more tempting than I wanted to admit. And I would feel like less of a creep than I did just standing there, staring at him.

I walked over to the bathtub and James moved toward the center, giving me room to climb in behind him. The tub was plenty big, but not quite big enough that two grown men could sit in it side by side without touching. I took my clothes off and sank against the back of the tub before reaching out, gently pulling him back against me.

To my surprise, he sank against my chest, laying the back of his head on my shoulder.

"Is this okay?" I asked quietly.

"Why wouldn't it be?"

James had always had a way of putting me at a loss for words in as few words as possible. I sighed, wrapping an arm around his waist, careful to avoid his wound. "No reason."

"It's comfortable," he murmured after around ten minutes of saying nothing. He was just laying there against me while I found myself counting the beats of his heart. I was far more invested in the continuation of that rhythm than I had realized until just then.

"Huh?" I asked.

"The water." He sighed. "I spent hours in the pool where I used to live with Silas. Just floating, staring up through the skylight. He found me once and thought I'd drowned myself."

I blew a puff of air through my nostrils. "What did he do?"

He didn't answer right away. Silas was always a touchy subject with him, even when we had been living in the same house. "I believe his exact words were, 'For fuck's sake, not in the pool.'"

It took a moment for me to process the callousness of that. "Yeah. Sounds like Silas."

"He sounded so annoyed," James said with a nostalgic chuckle. "But relieved, too. That's all I ever was to him, really. Somewhere between an asset and a liability. It was always just a matter of time before the balance tipped and I wasn't worth the expense."

I pulled my arms around him tighter, and his heart beat faster as his body grew stiffer. I leaned in, my nose pressed to the spot just beneath his ear, as I breathed in. "For what it's worth, you deserve better than someone who thought you'd offed yourself in his pool and was mildly inconvenienced."

"Do I?" he asked. "Because I think there are a lot of people who would disagree with you. Malcolm and his dead fiance included."

I bristled at the reminder of James's not-so-morally gray past. He was right, of course. I knew he had hurt more people than just the monsters he'd started out with. In the course of hunting the monsters, he had become one himself. Logically, I knew that, and maybe it really was cognitive dissonance making me want to believe there was a rhyme or reason to his madness. That there was some higher purpose to his dark deeds.

"Why did you do it?" I asked. "All the other people... it makes sense. Hell, I would have done the same thing if I were in your shoes, but Owen... he was innocent."

"Was he?" he asked boredly.

I looked down at him. "What do you mean?"

"Nothing," he said, standing to get out of the water and grabbing a robe hanging by the tub before he stepped out of it.

"Hey," I said, getting out after him. I followed him into the bedroom, leaving a trail of water behind as I came to a stop at the edge of the bed, where he was presently pulling back the covers to get in. "Stop."

"Stop what?" he asked, picking up one of the pillows to adjust it.

"Stop deflecting," I growled, taking his wrist in my hand. "Stop shutting down every time I try to talk to you."

"I'm bored," he said pointedly, staring me down. "You should be happy. Usually, when people bore me, I just kill them."

I gritted my teeth, vying for patience. "You're full of shit, you know that? You want me to believe this... this persona you've created that's Silas 2.0, but I don't."

"I told you to stop romanticizing me, Luca," he said with a bitter edge to his tone.

"There's a difference between romanticizing someone and trying to understand them," I countered. "And I don't buy for a second that a guy who'd risk his own life to rescue a stranger's kid is capable of killing an innocent guy in cold blood without a reason."

"I had a reason," he said with a shrug. "I wanted to punish Silas, and before your brother came along, the only way to do that was through Malcolm. To drive a wedge between them by taking the one thing Malcolm actually cared about other than himself."

"Bullshit," I snarled. "Maybe that was part of it, but that's not all of it. It doesn't match your MO."

"My MO?" he asked flatly. "And what is that?"

"Justice," I answered. "You never do anything you don't think is fair. And I'm not saying it *is* fair. I'm not saying it's right. All I'm saying is that somewhere inside your incredibly fucked-up brain, you're at the very least morally consistent."

His eyes narrowed and I could tell I'd struck a nerve. He jerked away from me. "I don't want to talk about this."

"Well, tough shit, because we're going to talk about it," I told him, stepping forward so he had no choice but to fall back onto the bed. I climbed onto it, putting my hands on the mattress on either side of him to keep him pinned without putting any physical pressure on him that might aggravate his wound.

A dangerous look came into James's eyes, but I could sense it was fear more than anything else. He was vulnerable right now, and he knew it, and as much as I wanted answers, I didn't want them at the expense of making him feel unsafe.

I reached out, slipping one hand into his hair, and he froze, staring up at me with widening eyes. "Just talk to me,

Chapter 22

James," I pleaded. "Please. Just this once, be honest, even if it's only with yourself."

He continued to stare at me for a few moments that felt like they lasted a lot longer than they could have in reality. When he finally spoke, his voice was devoid of every emotion but one—confusion. "Why does it matter?"

I paused to consider it, because that was a good question. Why *did* it matter why he had done what he had done?

"Because I..." I struggled to find the words. "Because I just need to know. I need to know the truth—*your* truth—even if it isn't what I want to hear."

James frowned. I could tell he hadn't expected that response, and he didn't seem quite sure how to answer. When he finally did, his voice was tight.

"He killed someone," he finally said.

I blinked. "Owen killed someone?"

"He was only seventeen," he muttered. "He'd been drinking at a party and hit a girl on his way home. He didn't stop, and she suffered for hours before she succumbed to her injuries. The police tracked him down later, but his father was a big shot lawyer. Important and rich enough to make sure Owen was tried as a juvenile. The case was thrown out on some conveniently 'missing' evidence. His record was sealed. I doubt even Malcolm knows about it."

I stared at him for a few moments, processing. "So that's why you killed him?"

"No," James said sharply. "That's how I justified it to myself. I killed him because I wanted to hurt Silas. I wanted an excuse."

"And if you hadn't found one?" I challenged. "Would you have done it, then?"

James didn't answer for a few moments. He just continued staring me down, his eyes boring holes into the center of my forehead because they refused to meet mine.

"I don't know," he finally said through his teeth. "Why does it even matter?"

"Because it does, James," I answered. "It matters because it means you're different. You think Silas ever needed a reason? You think Malcolm ever needs an excuse for any of the shit that he does? You're not like them, no matter how much you want to think you are."

"Why do you fucking care?" he cried. "Why does it matter to you if I'm like them or not?"

"Because I don't want to believe I'm falling in love with a monster!" I snapped.

The words were out of my mouth before I could stop myself. I froze and stared down at him, and he stared back. For a long while, neither of us said a word.

I wasn't sure there was anything to say.

23

JAMES

All I could do for a few moments was stare up at Luca in disbelief.

"Oh, you poor fool," I finally said. "You actually think you—"

I broke off as Luca crushed his lips to mine.

Pushing him away would've been the wise thing to do. The kind thing. But I had never been either.

I found myself returning the kiss, my tongue tangling with his, my body enveloped in his warmth. He kissed me aggressively before suddenly biting my neck as if he wanted to devour me whole. His touch sent shivers down my spine, and I could feel an insatiable hunger rising up within me—an urge that threatened to consume us both if we let it.

Luca's hands moved over every inch of my body, exploring and caressing and pulling me closer still. I clung to him tightly, feeling as though I were being pulled into an abyss of pure pleasure.

He was so different in bed. So demanding. So aggressive.

And I liked it. I liked that boring, safe Luca DiFiore had a wild side—maybe even a dark side—and I liked it even more that I was the one who brought it out of him.

Luca must have sensed my thoughts because he suddenly pulled back and looked into my eyes. His gaze was hot and primal, something wild lurking in the depths of his eyes that I hadn't seen before.

He leaned in again, biting down hard on my bottom lip this time. I gasped at the sudden pleasure-pain, feeling my knees go weak as he licked the spot to soothe it.

My heart beat faster as Luca stepped away for a moment and pulled open a drawer nearby. He smirked wickedly at me as he retrieved a tube of lubricant from it.

"Ah," he said, his voice low and laced with amusement. "Prepared, are we?"

"You don't need to be so smug. It's not as if I planned on inviting you here," I reminded him.

He laughed. "No, I guess you didn't," he said.

He moved closer and kissed down my neck, muttering into my skin. "Don't make me jealous."

I shivered at the suggestion, feeling a surge of heat between my legs. Luca must have felt this too, because his hands ran over my body more urgently now. His fingers teased and tantalized as they went lower and lower until I was almost unable to take it anymore.

Chapter 23

Self-control was not something I had ever lacked, but when it came to him, I found myself succumbing to his every desire.

He continued to kiss me, making my body ache for more before he finally stopped and moved away. I was about to complain until I felt his fingers spreading the lube around my asshole. He applied it generously, teasing me with his fingers as if he knew what I wanted even before I did.

I felt my breath catch in my throat as his fingers entered me, exploring and stretching me as they went deeper. His touch felt electric against my skin, sending waves of pleasure through my entire body that left me trembling in anticipation.

"Being gentle tonight, are we?" I taunted.

"You haven't really given me the chance before," he told me. "But you might like it."

At his hands, I was sure I would. But I wasn't ready to admit that any more than I was ready to process his little misguided declaration of love.

Fucking, I could handle.

Love? That was something else entirely.

I wasn't sure I even knew what it was like to be loved, let alone by someone like Luca. Someone good. It was a strange thought.

He continued to prepare me, his hands never leaving my body as he shifted around behind me. His fingers teased and tantalized, pushing deeper inside me until I could feel the pleasure, which was almost too much to bear. He moved slowly at first, stroking and exploring with his fingers until I was moaning and begging for more.

His touch was gentle but sure as he moved his fingers in and out of me faster and faster until I was on the brink of release. His other hand pressed firmly against my hip, steadying me as I rocked back against him, sending wave after wave of pleasure coursing through my body.

I could feel myself tensing up in anticipation, a tingly feeling radiating from deep within me that promised something more to come. Luca must have felt it, too, because he suddenly pulled his fingers out and I gasped in response.

He moved up between my legs, pushing them apart as he prepared to fuck me. His eyes glowed with desire and satisfaction at the sight of me spread before him.

We had fucked before, but there was something about this time that was different. It felt intimate, and that was the one thing that seemed capable of shaking my confidence.

Luca leaned in close, his lips ghosting over mine as he whispered in a gravelly voice, "You're my first, and I'm going to be yours."

I gave a dry laugh against his lips as he pressed against me, applying just enough pressure to make my hole ache without actually penetrating me. "I'm afraid you're a couple decades too late for that, pet."

"You're the first man I've ever been with," he continued, gazing down at me. "And I'm going to be the first person who makes love to you. Fucking doesn't count."

His words caught me off guard. He proceeded to ease his cock into me gently, inch by inch, until I was filled with him completely. He moved slowly at first, rocking against me as he built up a rhythm that left me gasping and moaning in pleasure.

I felt my body responding to his touch, the tension between us growing more intense with each thrust and caress. His hands held my hips firmly as he pushed himself deeper inside of me, and I could feel my orgasm starting to build, picking up from where I'd left off.

He pressed his lips to mine to swallow up a moan, his tongue exploring my mouth as he continued to fuck me passionately but gently, and I felt so vulnerable. Every stroke of his hips sent a wave of pleasure radiating through my body as I clung to him, lost in the sensations he was bringing out in me.

I buried my face in his neck, because I couldn't bear to let him see my face. Not when I was having such a hard time holding back what I was feeling, and what I was feeling was...

Confusion. It was dizzying, maddening, but all-consuming, too. He was right. This wasn't just fucking, it was something more. Something else entirely.

Something that scared the hell out of me, but I didn't want it to stop. Not just yet.

When he reached between us and started stroking my cock, I was sure I would break apart in an instant, but he kept going. His hands were gentle but firm and his touch was exquisite, as if he was worshiping my body with each caress.

He kept fucking me until I finally couldn't take it any longer and my orgasm washed over me like a tidal wave, leaving me shaking and trembling in its wake.

Luca kept stroking as the streams of come slipped through his fingers, his touch exquisitely, torturously gentle. Like he wasn't just touching a lover, but rather playing an instrument, and each caress drew new notes of pleasure from me.

He captured them with another kiss and finally released my cock when the sensation became too much. He started thrusting harder, faster, and I basked in the pleasurable aftershocks of orgasm, his cock pressing against my prostate each time he drove into me. It was torture and pure bliss.

I could feel Luca shuddering inside me as he followed me over the edge. The sensation of him coming filled me with a sense of satisfaction and completion, like something inside me had clicked back into place after being broken for so long.

When it was over, we lay there in each other's arms, both breathless and exhausted from what had just happened.

My head was spinning, but that was nothing compared to the tempest he had stirred within me.

"What the fuck was that?" I finally asked when I trusted myself to speak, staring up at him.

The bastard wore a smug smirk on his lips, knowing damn well he had just rocked my world.

"Making love," he said, taking my hand and kissing my fingertips. The tenderness of that gesture just added insult to injury. "What did you think?"

Chapter 23

I looked away, more flustered by his words—and everything that had just transpired between us—than I wanted to admit.

"This would all be so much simpler if I could just kill you," I muttered.

"You can," he said, kissing me once more before he eased out of me. I winced slightly, even though he was gentle in that, too. He rolled onto his side, pulling me against his chest. "Nothing's stopping you."

"Don't tempt me," I mumbled, burrowing into his side.

"You're surprisingly cuddly for a serial killer," he remarked.

"Fuck you."

"Still not satisfied?" he taunted. "Give me a minute and we'll go again."

"You're absurd," I said, shaking my head and smiling in spite of myself.

It was the truth. He was absurd, and I had a sinking suspicion I was actually beginning to like that.

So what the fuck did that make me?

24

LUCA

I woke up to an empty bed and rolled my eyes. The spot next to me had long grown cold, so there was no way of telling how long James had been awake.

Hell, he didn't even seem to need to sleep for more than a few hours a night.

I got out of bed and got dressed, walking downstairs. I probably should've been afraid he had gone MIA on me, and even after what had happened between us last night, I knew that would be a logical response. I wasn't, though. And I wasn't surprised when I found him downstairs, working at his computer with a massive mug of black coffee that was almost empty.

"How long have you been awake?" I asked with a yawn.

"Four hours, give or take," he answered.

I blinked, looking over at the clock on the display. "It's barely six in the morning. Do you even sleep?"

"Not much," he said, reaching for the mug.

Chapter 24

"Here," I said, taking it from him. "The least I can do is keep you fueled, I guess."

"Thank you," he said, seeming surprised.

"I don't know if you should be thanking me, considering you drink enough of this shit to power a small country."

"A city-state at best," he countered, turning back to the screen.

I sighed, coming back a few minutes later with a fresh cup I set in front of him. "There," I said. "What are you doing? Anything I can help with?"

"Not unless you've become a cryptologist on the astral plane," he replied.

I snorted. "I'm afraid I'm not. But that contact of Malcolm's does seem to know his stuff. If you're trying to hack into Lewis's systems or whatever, he might be able to help."

James finally looked up, raising an eyebrow. "'Hack into his systems'? Really?"

"Okay, so what are you doing?"

His eyes narrowed. "Technically, I am trying to 'hack into his systems,' but you make it sound so cliché."

I scoffed. "Sorry."

"In any case, Malcolm's contacts can't be trusted," said James.

"I know that, but I was talking about kidnapping him," I admitted.

He looked up at me again. "Kidnapping? Have I won you over to the dark side that easily?"

I smirked. "Well, you are good in bed."

"There's more where that came from, pretty boy," he said dryly, his eyes glinting with mischief as he took a sip of the coffee. "You're not bad at fucking either. Or making coffee. You are a shitty cook, though."

"Well, two out of three's not bad," I said, leaning down to kiss him. It somehow felt like an even more intimate gesture than anything we had done the night before, but that didn't put me off. It was the opposite. "Something's bothering you."

James's eyes widened slightly, as if the observation surprised him. "What makes you say that?"

"I don't know," I admitted. "Just a sense."

He didn't seem to know what to make of that, either. He finally looked away, staring at the numbers running across the screen. "I thought Lewis would have tried to contact us by now."

I took a moment to process that. Of course, every moment that passed without contact was a moment I spent torturing myself with what if, but hearing him say that brought it home on a whole other level.

"You don't think he's going to do it?" I asked.

"I think I'm not willing to risk that he won't," James answered. "We need to go on the offensive. At least as far as making contact goes."

"Okay, so how do we do that?" I asked. Putting my trust in someone else was difficult enough, let alone when it came

Chapter 24

to my son, but right now, James was the only person I *did* trust. I sure as hell couldn't trust Malcolm, or even Silas.

I certainly didn't trust them around James, and I had become protective of him as well, if I was being honest with myself.

"There's someone I've been thinking about reaching out to," he answered. "An old contact I think could prove useful as a go-between."

Anyone who was on civil enough terms with a man like Lewis to act as a go-between was automatically on my shit list, but we were desperate. "You know how to contact them?"

"I already did," he answered. "I'm taking a flight to meet him later today."

"You?" I asked, frowning. "Why are you talking like you're doing this alone?"

"Because I am," James said without hesitation. "This guy isn't exactly trustworthy. It's a Hail Mary."

"All the more reason you shouldn't be going alone," I said firmly.

He gave me a look I was becoming too familiar with. "As touching as your concern is, I've been doing these things myself for a long time."

"Yeah, and I meant what I said last night. You don't have to," I said, tilting his chin toward me. "It's my son. I'm going with you, James. End of story."

His eyes narrowed as he stared up at me. "There are six different ways I could render you unconscious right now. Easily."

"I'm sure there are," I said. "But you're not going to."

"And what makes you so sure of that?" he asked.

"For one thing, you're telling me rather than doing it," I replied.

He grunted in irritation.

"For another," I continued. "You know I'm right. You need back up. Right now, I'm the only option you have."

"What an unfortunate turn of events," he said with a weary sigh.

"I'll go get everything ready," I told him, heading back upstairs before he could change his mind.

25

JAMES

I highly doubted the man sitting next to me on the privately chartered jet had any idea just how much effort it had taken me to arrange for the last-minute transport when most of my usual connections weren't even available to me, thanks to being on the run from Silas and Malcolm. I doubted he was going to be much help if things with Thomas went south, for that matter, but he was right about one thing. I didn't have any other options.

At least he was eye candy for the ride.

I could tell he was a bundle of nerves throughout the two-hour flight, since he didn't say much and anxiety was just about the only thing capable of shutting a DiFiore up, as I had learned. A cock in the mouth would probably work, too, but I wasn't sure just how adventurous Luca was feeling.

When we finally landed, there was still another hour's drive to Thomas's mountain cabin. I had no doubt he had chosen it on purpose, because there was no prayer of getting a signal up there with any of the regular networks. It would make any coordinated efforts to hunt him down for his laundry list of crimes that much more difficult, and a man like Thomas was always thinking of his own hide, first and foremost.

"You let me do the talking," I told Luca as I parked the car I'd rented with a fake ID and a fraudulent credit card on the side of the road leading up the mountainside in a truly nauseating tangle of twists and curves. "You're there for backup, nothing more."

"Yeah, yeah," Luca muttered, checking the gun beneath his jacket as if it was going to have disappeared over the last few minutes. "We've been over it."

"That's never stopped a DiFiore from interfering before," I told him.

"I'm not my brothers," he said pointedly. "And I'm not going to do anything that would risk the plan. You're in charge."

I nodded, remotely satisfied with his reassurance. We'd see if it lasted in the heat of the moment.

"We've got a hike ahead of us," I warned him, pulling on my gloves as I got out of the car. "Thomas was specific about parking at the foot of the mountain."

"This guy is paranoid, isn't he?" he asked, trudging through the snow after me.

"You have no idea," I said flatly. "But it pays to be paranoid when people are trying to kill you. Now be quiet. I'm sure he has the area bugged."

Luca grunted in acknowledgment.

Chapter 25

We walked together in silence until the massive house built into the mountainside came into view. It was positively gargantuan, with a huge stone facade looming out of the snow-capped mountain that encased it. I could just make out a few dark windows, their glass reflecting the setting sun. Thomas had truly made something extraordinary here. The wraparound porch was surrounded by tall evergreen trees and several large snow drifts, and I could see Thomas leaning on the railing, watching us through a pair of binoculars.

Paranoid, indeed.

He disappeared inside as we drew closer. He looked perfectly at ease as he came out of the mansion to greet us a few moments later, a smile on his face. He appeared to be an unsuspecting man in his early- to mid-forties with graying hair and deceptively kind eyes. And he was jovial enough on the surface to match his hapless appearance.

"Hello, James," Thomas said in a pleasant tone, nodding to me as he stood by. Subtle as they were, I immediately picked out the three snipers stationed at various points around the chalet, and I was sure there were at least half a dozen other guards waiting in case one of us made a wrong move.

I was also keenly aware of exactly where Luca stood at my side, approximately two and a half feet to my left. I already had a plan for covering him if Thomas or his men turned on us, but our chances of walking away from this were less than one percent if shit went down, so keeping an eye on Luca was a much more efficient use of my energy.

"Thomas," I said, nodding to him. "You've done well for yourself."

He looked around the property, smiling faintly. "I'm mostly retired these days. Last I heard, so were you. Retired from life, at any rate."

I blew a puff of air through my nostrils. "What can I say? Rumors of my demise have been greatly exaggerated."

"Indeed," he remarked. "Imagine my surprise when a ghost from the past shows up asking about Lewis Capello, the one man who could make *me* disappear without a trace. And he wants me to facilitate an exchange, no less."

"Not an exchange," I countered. "I just need you to make the connection. We lost touch."

"Sounds like a deal went bad," he remarked.

"Maybe," I agreed. "But I can assure you, he wants to hear from me."

"Considering you killed his brother, I'm sure that's true," Thomas replied. "But there is the question of whether I want to be involved in making that reunion happen."

"Name your price," I said, hoping that keeping a level head would encourage Luca to do the same. "You know I'm good for it."

So far, Luca was complying with my instructions that he was not to intervene in the negotiations in any way, shape, or form, but he was a DiFiore, and I knew better than to think there was any guarantee his emotions wouldn't get the better of him.

Especially considering they had before. Plenty of times. That was half the reason he was so much fun.

"As you can see, it's not about money for me anymore," Thomas said, looking around pointedly once more. "I only take on passion projects these days, and I'm afraid that the line of business the Capellos are in just doesn't cut it. Which makes me curious as to what business *you* have with them. I seem to recall you being rather averse to the flesh trade yourself the last time we met."

"I am," I said, trying to keep my voice neutral. "But it's a unique situation."

"It always is," Thomas said with a wide grin.

He had me over a barrel, and he knew it. I could also tell from the way he kept glancing at Luca that he knew the other man was a potential weak spot as well.

Whether Thomas planned on double-crossing me or not, it was the kind of thing you noticed naturally in this line of work. You were always looking for the weakness to exploit. The cracked door that could be forced open in a pinch.

"Lewis has his son," I finally said, ignoring Luca's look of dismay. I had told him to keep his mouth shut, but I knew what to say and when—and what *not* to say. Thomas was the one who held all the cards at the moment, and there was no point in denying that for ego's sake. Weakness, too, could be exploited as a strength in the right hands. "And Lewis wants me in exchange."

The curiosity that lit the broker's eyes immediately told me my strategy was working. "I see. What an interesting turn of events," he said, his gaze drifting over to Luca with intensifying interest. "And may I ask what you're hoping to gain from this transaction?"

"Either I kill Lewis and get the kid back that way, or Lewis gets me and he gets the kid anyway," I said, nodding in Luca's direction. "You get paid either way. It'll be your easiest job yet. Perhaps you can even expand the porch."

Thomas scoffed a laugh. "Until things go sideways, you fail at your little rescue mission, Lewis kills you, and then he turns on me."

"All you're doing is making the connection," I told him. "And don't forget, I've come back from the dead before. Between me and the Capellos, it's one to zero. I suppose you just need to figure out if those are good enough odds to bet on."

Thomas's lips curved into a smirk. "Well played."

Luca looked like he wanted to tell me off for acting threatening, but he kept his mouth shut. Good boy.

"I'll make the point of contact," Thomas said after a moment's contemplation. "But that's all. I will give you a phone, and I will give Lewis the number to that phone. You will wire me the money by the end of the day. End of."

"That's all I'm asking for," I said.

"Then we have a deal," Thomas remarked. He nodded to one of his men, and my hand instinctively twitched for my gun as the guard moved, but he simply went inside. Ten minutes later, he returned with a small black bag and walked up to us to hand it to me.

I opened the bag and took out the old-school flip cell phone. I opened it, checking for any sign that it had been tampered with.

"It's untraceable, of course," said Thomas. "But you're welcome to go down to the base of the mountain where you can get a signal and wait until he contacts you. I expect it won't be long once I make the call."

"Thank you," I said, slipping the phone into my pocket. "We'll be out of your hair after that."

"Much obliged," Thomas replied with a closed-mouth smile.

I turned and motioned for Luca to follow me back down the mountain to where the car was waiting. I could feel we were being watched from the woods, and a glance over my shoulder revealed the camouflaged shoulder of at least one sniper. I knew there were plenty more where he came from, too.

"That went well," Luca said, glancing over me. "I think."

"We'll see when the phone rings," I said, slipping into the car to wait with him.

Even once we'd had the heat running for a minute, I could still see my breath in the air.

"You think it's safe here?" he asked.

"Absolutely not," I answered. "There's a chance Thomas just sent our location directly to Lewis."

"Seriously?"

"There's always a chance," I told him. "But it's not likely. I've known Thomas for years, and his bullshit about being retired aside, he has a reputation to uphold. You can't be a broker if you can't be trusted to be fair to both sides."

"Even if one side is a fucking sick freak," he said disdainfully.

"I said fair, I didn't say moral," I told him, keeping an eye on the treeline.

"Fair enough." He sighed.

The phone buzzed in my hand just then, and the display lit up. I stared down at the restricted number. "Looks like Thomas came through," I remarked. I brought the phone to my ear and answered. "Hello."

"James," Lewis said in a deceptively warm tone. "So good to finally hear your voice again. And here I thought you'd run off on me."

"You have my number," I told him. "And yet you haven't called. What's a girl to think?"

He gave a low chuckle. "Your number was compromised."

"You know better than that. I have my ways."

"My apologies for underestimating you," he said, his voice dripping with disdain. "I won't make the same mistake again. But I'd rather not run the risk of communicating on a compromised line all the same. Now, why don't you give me a clean number, and you can ditch that burner phone where you're at? I know you don't like to stay in one place for long."

"Since you asked," I said. I rattled off the number of a line I knew for certain he couldn't trace.

"Wonderful," he replied. "I prefer doing business directly. No middleman. That said, why don't you put me on with DiFiore, since I know you're not calling of your own free will."

"Actually, you're wrong," I said. "I'm the one calling the shots now, but the deal is still on. Me in exchange for the kid. You just need to name the time and place."

Luca stared at me in confusion, but a look was enough to silence him. For now.

"Interesting," Lewis murmured. "Why don't you tell me what it is about this kid that has you willing to throw yourself on the pyre? Or are you just that eager to see me?"

"We've had a score to settle for years, Lewis," I answered. "You're the one who chose to use a child as a shield to hide behind, but he doesn't need to factor into it. You want me? Then let's do this face-to-face, man-to-man. Because as far as I'm concerned, you and your brother are a set, and I don't like having a partial collection of trophies. I still have his index finger bone, you know. I keep it in a little jar. I've got the perfect place in mind for yours, too, although I might settle for a trophy a bit further down."

Lewis gave a low, dangerous chuckle. "Big words. I hope you're ready to deliver."

A second later, the phone buzzed and I looked down to find that he had texted me two sets of coordinates.

"The first location is where little Timothy will be, if and when you show up at the second location," said Lewis.

"Lovely," I said. "What should I wear?"

"Doesn't matter," said Lewis. "You won't be wearing it for long. You just come at your earliest convenience. I'll be waiting."

He hung up and I stared down at the burner phone for a moment before tossing it out into the snow.

"Drive," I told Luca.

"Are we not going to talk about that?" Luca demanded. "What the fuck do you mean, you're trading yourself for—"

"I said drive," I snapped.

His eyes narrowed, and I could tell he wanted to argue. For a few seconds, he seemed like he was going to, but then he cursed under his breath and pulled out onto the narrow mountain road. "We're not done talking about this."

I knew we weren't. But my mind was made up all the same.

26

JAMES

"It's simple," I said, loading a black duffel bag with enough guns to arm a small militia. I was glad I kept so many toys at this safe house. "We've gone over it half a dozen times."

"Yeah, and I'm still missing the part where you and Timothy walk out of this with me. Together," Luca countered.

"That's because there isn't one," I said with a shrug. "I'm the one going to the island."

"Not alone, you're not," Luca insisted. It was kind of cute he thought he had a say in any of this. Naïveté was one of his most endearing qualities by far. "Look, I know you don't trust Malcolm, and neither do I, but he doesn't have to be involved in any of this. We can get Silas to help and we have a drop point. He can send an army."

"You don't think that's exactly what Lewis is expecting?" I asked. "He's already going to be gun shy after the last time. Any deviation from the plan and your son is at risk."

"I know that," he said through his teeth. "You don't think I know that?"

"I don't think you're acting rationally right now," I told him. "So I'm not giving you a choice."

"That's bullshit," he growled.

"No, it's actually quite straightforward," I said. "You go to the drop site with Silas and the others. That, he'll be expecting. And it won't be a threat, considering he'll be at the island. With me."

"And you'll be alone," he argued. "As usual."

"It's what I'm good at."

"This is suicide," Luca said bitterly. "You know that."

"I'm not planning on dying," I told him.

"No, you're planning on killing him, whatever it takes, even if dying is a part of that."

There was no point in denying it. He knew it, and I knew it. I just didn't want to admit it for some reason.

"You can't do this, James," he said firmly. "I'm not letting you do this."

"You're not being reasonable."

"No," he snapped. "Maybe I'm fucking not, but who gives a shit about reasonable? Not everything has to be logical, James. The way I feel about you sure as fuck isn't, but that doesn't mean it isn't real. It doesn't mean it isn't worth fighting for."

I stared at him for a moment, blinking. "Are you still on your bullshit about loving me?"

"It's not bullshit," he said, closing the distance between us to pin me against the wall. "It's the truth, even if I'm the only one of us who's not too much of a coward to admit it."

"You've been spending too much time around Malcolm," I told him.

He blew a puff of air through his nostrils. "If there's one thing I can admire that prick for, it's the fact that he would do anything to protect what's his. No matter what you think of me, I'm going to do the same."

"Yours," I murmured, absently reaching up to touch his face against my better judgment. "Is that what you think I am?"

"That's what I want you to be," he said without hesitation, holding my gaze. "I'm going to do whatever it takes to protect my son, but I'm not going to sacrifice you. Me, on the other hand? I'll protect you both, even if it costs me my life."

"Yes," I said quietly, looking him over. "I'm afraid you would."

He stared at me for a moment in confusion. "Don't."

"Don't what?" I asked.

"Don't look at me like that," he said. "Like you're planning something. Like you're planning on running off on your own. Always on your fucking own."

"That's the way it always has been," I reminded him.

"It doesn't have to be that way," he insisted. "You don't have to be alone, and you don't want to be. I know you don't because you could've been that day at the docks. You could've just left me there, and no one, not even Silas, would have blamed you, but you didn't. You stuck your neck out on the line for me, someone who had fucked you over, and now you're trying to do it again. Because you're more afraid of letting someone in, letting someone help you, than you are of fucking dying."

The most annoying part was, he wasn't wrong. Not about that, at least. But he was wrong about me being afraid of letting someone in. I had already done that without even realizing it, and the consequences were as dire as I had always thought they would be. Consequences I was about to choose willingly nonetheless.

"I'm not letting you go, James," he told me, his eyes fierce and steady.

And I knew he meant it. I should have walked away right then and there. I should have knocked him out, which would be a hell of a lot easier when his guard was down, but I could have done it right then regardless. I'd already prepared a capsule when we'd first come here just in case I needed to get him out of the way. It wouldn't kill him. It was just a sedative, but it was strong enough that it would keep him down for the count long enough to give me time to escape.

In the beginning, I'd expected I would have to use it because he would try to double cross me again, but now, it was going to be put to a very different use. I just couldn't bring myself to do it.

Not just yet.

It was ironically one of the most selfish things I had ever done, but I wanted a little bit more time with him. Just another moment.

I leaned in and pressed my lips against his, and he didn't hesitate to pull me closer as the kiss quickly turned passionate. His arms slipped around my waist, pulling me into his embrace as our mouths moved together in a frenzied rhythm.

He pulled away slowly and looked down at me intently with those dark eyes of his. His gaze seared into me, conveying so much more than words ever could have.

Luca took my hand and led me into the bedroom without another word. The moment we made it to the bed, he pushed me down and kissed me again. In that single kiss, that single moment, it all converged—the brutal passion that had characterized our earliest interactions, and the tenderness that had only unfolded recently between us.

It was a perfect blend, and it felt like coming home.

He undressed me slowly, exploring every inch of me with his eyes and hands. His touch was gentle, yet powerful, and it filled me with a longing I hadn't known I could feel.

Luca's body pressed against mine as our movements became more urgent and intense. He lowered his naked body on top of mine, being careful to avoid my stitches, and pressed against me. His fingers laced through mine as he pinned my hands to the mattress.

His mouth found mine again, then my neck as he worked his way down my body. I let out a deep moan as his tongue teased and caressed me in all the right places. His breath was hot against my skin, sending shivers down my spine.

He deftly reached for a bottle of lube without breaking the kiss and slipped two slick fingers into me. I moaned in bliss as he found my spot and started pumping his fingers in and out, building up to a delicious rhythm that had me trembling with pleasure and my hips rocking in time.

He slowly withdrew his hand and kissed his way back up my torso, finally settling between my legs. He slowly guided his cock to my entrance, then pushed himself in, inch by glorious inch.

I gasped as he filled me completely and began to move inside of me. His thrusts were deep yet gentle as we both found a rhythm that felt perfect for us. Our bodies moved together in harmony, sending waves of pleasure throughout me every time he buried himself to the hilt inside me.

Luca shifted slightly so he could reach down to cup my balls in one hand while the other toyed with the sensitive skin on my crown. His fingers were electric against me, setting off a thousand tiny sparks that lit up every nerve ending in their path.

My orgasm was building quickly now, and before I knew it, I was screaming out Luca's name as I came. He shuddered and tightened his grip on my balls as he followed me over the edge, spilling himself inside of me in a torrent of pleasure.

We collapsed onto the bed, our breathing slow and heavy as we lay there together in blissful satisfaction. Luca reached down to caress my cheek and looked into my eyes with such gentle passion that it almost overwhelmed me. No one had ever looked at me like that before.

"Are you going to let me say it this time?" he asked, his voice still husky from exertion.

I sighed, looking away from him. "If you must."

I saw a ghost of a smile on his lips as he bent down, his breath grazing the stubble on my throat as he brushed his lips against my neck.

"I love you," he whispered, making me shudder again.

Those words filled me with so many conflicting emotions, disbelief chief among them. But as much of a skeptic as I was about most things, I found myself wanting to believe his declaration, as foolhardy as it was.

I didn't know what to say, so I slipped my fingers into his hair and pressed a soft kiss to his forehead. He smiled and kissed me in return, holding me tight against him. We stayed like that for a while, neither of us speaking as the weight of those three little words settled around us.

"I'm going to take a shower," he murmured into my hair. "Care to join me?"

"I think I'll stay here," I replied, kissing his cheek as he stood to leave.

I lay there alone in the bed, listening to the water running in the next room as I bathed in a thousand different feelings I thought had been lost forever. Love was such an ambiguous emotion. No matter how often it was discussed or written about, it still remained so difficult to define.

But whatever this was between us—the passion we shared and the tenderness we had developed—it felt real and true. Even though I couldn't bring myself to say it out loud, I knew that deep down inside my heart, it held those same three little words for Luca as well.

But actions had always meant more than words to me, anyway, and if I couldn't do this, I didn't deserve him. I didn't deserve any of this.

I reached into the pocket of my fallen clothing and popped the small capsule under my tongue as I heard the shower turn off, and I prepared to do what I knew I had to do. I felt a strange sense of calm about it as Luca came out and rejoined me in bed, gathering me into his arms.

I kissed him once more, deepening the kiss and digging my nails into his flesh so violently he didn't seem to notice as I shoved the capsule down over the back of his tongue and felt him swallow instinctively.

He stilled for a moment, and I saw the confusion in his eyes as he tried to comprehend what had just happened.

I watched the confusion in his eyes turn to realization, then betrayal, then panic, all in such quick succession it might as well have been one emotion.

"No," he said through his teeth, pushing me off him as he got up to shove his fingers down his throat.

"Don't try to fight it. It's quick acting once it comes in contact with stomach acid," I said, offering him the glass of water on the table. "It won't harm you, but it'll keep you from following me."

He took the glass, seemingly out of instinct, before tossing it aside and trying to stand. He failed to stay on his feet and fell back onto the edge of the bed. "Don't do this, James. Please," he begged.

"I'm sorry," I said quietly. The fact that he wasn't freaking out thinking I'd just poisoned him somehow made me feel even guiltier.

He was actually beginning to trust me. All the more reason I had to betray him. For his own good.

I could count on one hand the number of times I had told someone I was sorry and meant it, but I did. I meant it so much it was a pain, twisting and gnawing deep inside of me. "When this is all over, if I'm still around and you still want me, then we can try. You can say your pretty words, and I'll say them in return, but until then, it's all just poetry. It's fantasy. And I'm sure you've read enough bedtime fairy tales to Timothy to know that things never end happily between Prince Charming and the monster."

"James," Luca gritted out, reaching for me. I let him grasp my wrist, because I wanted to touch them one last time. One touch that wasn't tinged with a lie, even if it was poisoned with the aftermath of betrayal.

I held his hand until the light faded from his eyes and the strength left his body. He collapsed in my lap in peaceful slumber that would last more than long enough for me to leave him the coordinates and get away. Long enough for me to get too far for him to do anything but accept the only proper role he had in this, which was being there to rescue his son—an innocent boy who never should've had a part in any of this, and was most likely never going to be aware of mine.

It was for the best. He would have enough trauma from this whole ordeal, but with Luca and the rest of the family there to love and support him through it, he would heal. In time, knowing how plastic the brain was at his age, he would forget it altogether.

He didn't need one more monster in his closet.

27

LUCA

I woke up with a pounding migraine, hardly able to feel my limbs. It took a long time for me to come to enough to remember how I had gotten back to the cabin, and why James wasn't there. As soon as I did, I panicked and leaped out of bed, my head spinning so badly that I stumbled across the room.

Shit.

A phone I didn't recognize was conspicuously accessible on the nightstand, but I knew trying to contact James was a lost cause. He had already premeditated this, and his mind wouldn't change no matter what I said or did.

Knowing what he was trying to do—the fact that he was trying to protect me—made it feel less like betrayal, but it was all the more infuriating.

He was going to get himself killed. The thought was more terrifying than I could even get my head around. I knew what I had to do, though.

I had to call Silas.

Fuck, this was bad.

Each ring of the phone echoed in my ears, pure torture, but I was never more relieved than I was when he picked up.

"James," he said, his voice tense with suspicion and anger. Of course he thought I was being held hostage or something. Why wouldn't he?

"It's me," I said. "I need your help."

"Luca?" His tone relaxed immediately. "Where are you? Are you all right?"

"I'm fine," I muttered, reaching into my pocket for the sheet of paper James had left. "I'm at one of James's safe houses, but it doesn't matter. I'm texting you a set of coordinates, and you need to have a team ready. Lewis is going to drop Timothy off there."

"How do you know this?" Silas demanded. I could hear the others in the background, and I was pretty sure one of them was Enzo. "Where is James right now?"

My stomach tightened into a knot as I worked up the answer. "He's gone," I said, my voice growing hoarse. "And I'm going after him."

Silas fell silent for a few moments. "You're *what*?"

"If I send you another set of coordinates, can you get me there?" I asked. Even though James had given me Timothy's coordinates, I'd memorized both sets just in case. It looked like that was the right decision, all things considered.

Chapter 27

"What? Luca, you're not making any sense," Silas said. "Just tell me where you—"

"Answer me, or I'll figure it out myself."

He paused long enough that I wasn't sure what he was going to say. "Yes," he finally said. "But you need to think about what it is you're saying. This is James we're talking about."

"I know," I snapped. "That's why I'm going." I hung up before I sent him the other coordinates.

It was a matter of a couple of hours before I heard the choppers coming to pick me up, and I'd spent the time going through the house, gathering weapons and other things I thought I might be able to use on my mission.

I wasn't sure what I was going to do when Malcolm showed up. Probably kill him, which was why I was relieved when it was only Silas and a team of his agents.

He immediately dispatched them to search the safe house, then came over to meet me.

"There you are," he muttered. "Judging from how you were on the phone, I was afraid you wouldn't be here when we arrived."

"If I had a faster way to the island, I wouldn't have been," I admitted.

Silas's eyes narrowed, so I knew he hadn't just given up on talking me out of my plan. He'd simply decided to wait to argue in person. "I'm not going to pretend like I know what's been happening, and I understand you're upset about what happened at the docks. What Malcolm did was out of line, and trust me, I'm seeing to it—but you can't just take this into your own hands."

"I'm not. James already has," I said pointedly. "And that's the only reason my kid is still alive right now. Not because of you, and actively in spite of Malcolm. Because of James. And I'm not leaving him in the hands of that psycho, so you're either going to help me, or you're going to get out of my fucking way."

Silas stared at me for a few seconds in disbelief, and to be fair, it was hard to imagine many people talked to him like that. Even I would have been hesitant on any other occasion, but I was too focused on the mission at hand right now to give a shit what he did to me.

"God, Enzo was right," he finally muttered, looking away. I wasn't sure what to make of the implication that they had been talking about me behind my back, but that was the least of my worries right now.

"Are you going to help me or not?"

"I'll do what I can," said Silas. "But the coordinates you sent me... That island is off the radar in more ways than one. I won't be able to contact you when you're there, and from the intel I managed to gather, there's only one way in and one way out. I can send a team, but Lewis will have the entire island monitored and protected, and if that fails, he has a host of human hostages he can use as a shield. I can't risk sending an entire army in there, which is exactly what it would take to guarantee a clean extraction without massive casualties. Your son is far from the only innocent he's taken."

My stomach churned at the thought, but it was all the more reason I wanted to get my hands around Lewis's throat at the first opportunity I had. "I know the risks," I muttered. "I'll find James, and I'll get him out."

"And you're sure you know what you're doing?" Silas asked, eyeing me intently. "You're sure he's worth it?"

The question pissed me off, even though logically, I understood why he was asking it. He and I had very different perspectives on James, and we always would. But between the two of us, I was willing to bet that I was the only one who actually saw James for who he was.

"Absolutely," I said.

Silas breathed a deep sigh. "I'm going with you, then. It will have to be a small team. More than five and the risk of exposure is too great. If the Cappelo family's 'business' is anything like I imagine, there are many powerful people who would do whatever it takes to make sure what happens on the island stays there, and I think it's obvious enough that we can't trust the officials."

"Yeah," I said bitterly. "I gathered that from the company the freak keeps."

"We could use Malcolm," Silas said in a tone that made it clear he knew exactly what my reaction to that suggestion was going to be.

"Malcolm can go fuck himself," I snarled.

Silas rolled his eyes. "He's not who you want handling negotiations, but when it comes to killing off the radar, there's no one better to have at your side."

"Except he's got a vendetta against the man we're trying to rescue," I replied.

"For good reason," Silas said, raising an eyebrow.

I gritted my teeth. I really wasn't going to get into everything about Owen right now, and I knew that wouldn't change Silas's mind anyway. But the more time we spent arguing, the more time James was alone with Lewis.

"Fine," I said through my teeth. "But keep him in line, or I fucking will."

"Look at you," Silas said in a smug tone. "For a guy who's always had one foot out of the family business, you're actually starting to sound like someone who belongs in this world."

"Let's just move," I said, walking past him toward the chopper. "We've wasted enough time already."

Every second that passed, I felt like another part of me was missing, and if there was one fucking thing I'd learned in all this bullshit, it was that love was at its most painful in absence.

28

JAMES

The island air was thick and oppressive that night, and with each humid breath I took into my lungs, it felt like mildew was growing inside me. The wild nature around me was objectively splendid, but the man who had commandeered it had tainted its beauty, turning it cold and sinister.

There had been a fishing boat waiting to pick me up on the mainland, and I had gone willingly once I'd been shown footage proving Silas's men had indeed picked up Timothy. The grizzled old sailor hadn't said so much as a word as we sailed across dark waters, and I imagined he knew well enough to ask as few questions as possible in his line of work.

I checked my watch. It was getting late and I had been waiting for over an hour now. My patience was beginning to wear thin, but I knew this, too, was a part of Lewis's game.

He wasn't even the one who showed up first. The four men who came out of the jungle, clad in black military surplus gear and holding assault rifles, surrounded me without a word. Before long, Lewis decided to show his face. The resemblance to his dead brother was uncanny.

If all went according to plan, they would soon have something else in common.

"There you are," Lewis said in an unnervingly warm tone, holding his arms outstretched as he approached me. I remained always conscious of the two barrels pointed at my back. "Welcome to the island. The family business."

"Yes, it's quite the setup you've got here," I said boredly, looking around. "I suppose if you can't hack it in arms dealing, trading in flesh has its perks."

Lewis's lip curled back into a dangerous smirk. "Still fiery as ever. That's good. It'll be all the more satisfying to break you."

"And here I thought you brought me here to kill me," I remarked.

"Now where's the fun in that?" he asked. "Of course, that was my plan in the beginning. But we've been through so much together, even if this is the first time we've officially met. Killing you just felt so... anticlimactic. Don't you think?"

"Yeah," I muttered. "Wouldn't want that."

He just smiled and nodded to the men behind me. "Go on. Take him to the auction house. Make sure he's been adequately prepared for this evening. We've got a very special night ahead of us."

"I can't wait," I said flatly.

Chapter 28

There was a dangerous gleam in Lewis's eyes. He was everything I had expected and more.

The guards bound my arms behind my back and led me over to an all-terrain vehicle waiting at the edge of the jungle. They shoved me into the back, and as the vehicle took off, I stared at the shoreline and couldn't help but let my mind drift far beyond it.

Timothy was safe. By now, he was presumably with Luca, and if he wasn't home yet, he soon would be.

That was all that mattered.

It occurred to me that I had just traded my life for a boy I had never met, and I never would. The thought made me feel a strange pang in the center of my chest.

I had never cared about anyone other than Silas, and now, I found myself caring about a perfect stranger, simply because of who he was to another man who might as well have been a stranger to me. Luca didn't know me, not really. The fact that he thought he loved me was proof enough of that.

But what did I feel for him? I still wasn't sure. I had spent so many years in pure obsession over Silas that I had just assumed that was love, but what I had grown to feel for Luca over such a short time... The intensity of it made what I felt for Silas pale in comparison, but it was similar enough in many ways that I had to wonder. And yet, how could it be love if it didn't leave me feeling empty and aching?

I decided it didn't matter. It never would.

Whether it was love or not, whether I was even capable of love that wasn't tinged with wickedness, it was a moot point.

In any case, I cared enough about Luca to know his world was infinitely better without me in it.

Better. Safer. Saner.

He didn't even want his child being involved in the comparatively tame DiFiore family business, and if I somehow escaped Lewis by some miracle—or the exact opposite—the demons from my past were plentiful. And that was to say nothing of the fact that I was the worst among them.

The car stopped behind what looked like an old theater nestled in the center of the jungle, only it had to be relatively new. These people were nothing if not ostentatious.

God, I hated them. I knew I wasn't leaving this island alive, but I was going to drag as many of these fuckers to hell with me as I possibly could. I might as well give my life some meaning, even if it was only in its final moments.

And killing Lewis, if nothing else, certainly counted as giving my life purpose. It was as if it had all converged to this point. Like it was fate from the very beginning.

This was what I deserved. It was where I had been headed for as long as I could remember.

To my surprise, once we arrived at the auction house, I wasn't dragged into a torture chamber, but rather locked inside a large and well-appointed room. The fact that there was a bed made my stomach churn with thoughts of what Lewis planned on doing to me before he got his final revenge, whatever form that happened to take.

As far as I had been able to gather from my research into him and his life, he wasn't even interested in men, but that kind of thing hardly mattered. It was a game of power, nothing less and nothing more.

I was left on the edge of the bed in the room for a few hours, give or take, before they sent in two new guards. One looked like a teenager, and he couldn't have been far beyond eighteen. I could tell from the nervous air about him that he knew who and what I was, or at least enough to be appropriately wary.

He had probably come to this island under very different circumstances, and I wouldn't have been surprised if he had simply aged out of being useful to his captors in one regard, so they had appointed him to a different role. The prisoner becoming the warden was far from an uncommon turn of events in this world.

"So, where am I headed?" I asked, focusing on the young guard, since the other was seemingly made of stone.

The blond boy looked immediately on edge now that I had spoken to him. He glanced at the other guard, who just shrugged and said nothing.

"It doesn't matter," the boy said, tossing a stack of clothing on the bed beside me. "Just put these on. We'll deal with your necklace once a technician figures out a way to get it off without killing you."

"I can't very well do that with my hands tied behind my back, now, can I?" I challenged.

He hesitated, swallowing audibly as he looked me over. The other guard rolled his eyes and took out his keys, stalking over with great bravado. He was unnecessarily rough as he unclasped the restraints behind my back, and while I probably could have reached for his gun, I knew even if I killed them both, there was a small army waiting for me outside that door. I would never get to Lewis alive, let alone make it off the island—and while I had made my peace with dying, I wasn't ready to go down without a fight.

I changed into the three-piece suit that fit me perfectly, wondering what Lewis was playing at. I figured I would find out soon enough, and it was clear my guards weren't interested in talking.

They stayed on either side of me, leading me toward the stairwell in the back hallway. I took care to map out my surroundings so I'd be prepared if and when the chance to escape presented itself.

The place was larger than it had seemed from the outside, and I realized on further inspection that my first hunch had been right. This was definitely some kind of repurposed theater.

They led me upstairs to a private box overlooking the empty amphitheater below. The theater itself was circular, surrounding a large stage presently covered with two massive red curtains. When I thought about what it might be used for, my stomach churned with enough disgust and rage that I had to try not to think about it to keep my cool.

The radio chatter coming from the comms on either guard's hips picked up suddenly, and the older one muttered something about a perimeter check into his before turning to the boy. "Watch him. I'll be right back."

"Where are you going?" the boy protested, rightfully alarmed.

Chapter 28

"The guests are arriving," the other guard said impatiently. "Boss wants me to scan the area first. You got a gun, so use it, and if you're too chickenshit to do that, Miller's got you covered." He raised his hand and looked across the theater.

The next instant, a red dot appeared in the center of my chest. I followed the trajectory of the light to another box, and even though I couldn't see anyone in the shadows, I knew Miller was probably far from the only one with his eyes—and his sights—trained on me.

The boy seemed to calm down, not that he had much of a choice when his partner was already leaving.

"Must be rough," I said after a moment. I could feel the tension pouring off the kid.

He glanced sideways at me, both hands on his weapon. "What is?" he asked warily.

"I'm sure you came here bound and gagged in the back of a truck," I answered. "You probably thought you were getting out when you climbed out of the pit. And then he sticks you with a shit job like this."

I could tell from the look in his eyes that I had assessed his position correctly. They hardened a moment later. "You don't know shit. Shut up."

"You know he's never going to let you go, don't you?" I asked. "I don't know what they told you, but after all the things you've seen and all the shit they've done to you, you're never going to be free. You're going to spend the rest of your life putting yours on the line for a man who sees you as worth less than the shit in the treads of his shoes, always telling yourself that eventually, there will come a time when it's over. A time when you can be free, but the second you take that first step into the light, you'll end up with a bullet between your eyes."

The boy's eyes narrowed, but I could see the fear overtaking his anger. "I'm not leaving," he said through his teeth. "It doesn't matter."

"You're not, or you can't?" I challenged.

His jaw clenched and he looked down at the empty theater below. "My sister is here," he said quietly. "Lewis says he won't sell her off the island if I do what he says. Five years, and we're both out."

"Ah," I said in a knowing tone. "And you believe him."

Indignation flashed in his eyes. I was being a condescending asshole, and that was on purpose. Pride was as effective of a weakness to prey on as anything. Especially when it was pride in someone's ability to protect those they loved.

"Just shut up," he said through his teeth. "Or I'll make you."

I shrugged apathetically, knowing when it was time to back off. The boy was weak, but poor trigger discipline and a shaky hand were as dangerous as a cunning killer any day. Sometimes even more so.

I had been looking for a weakness to exploit, though, and I might have just found it.

I said nothing as the sounds of activity began to fill the auction house below. There were people filing into the seats, all of them wearing masks with the appearance of animals like some sort of twisted masquerade.

Chapter 28

The hedonists were so fucking cliché. Most of them were men, but there were a few women in the mix, too. I had no doubt that behind those masks lurked quite a few faces I would recognize, and not all of them from the underworld.

The guard had been watching the crowd below, glancing my way every so often, but when he froze and his expression shifted, I didn't even need to look over my shoulder to know that his boss had arrived.

I turned to find that Lewis was there, sure enough, walking toward me.

"Sorry to keep you waiting," Lewis said, sinking into the seat next to me. He waved to the guard. "Go wait outside."

"Yes, sir," the boy said, taking his rifle and walking out of the private box seat. He pulled the door shut behind him, and I didn't hear a lock.

"It's quite a packed house," I remarked. "Is it a special occasion?"

"Of course," Lewis said. "You didn't think I'd waste your time, did you?"

I snorted. "No, of course not."

"It's the biannual auction," he said. "It would seem you're just in time. Imagine that."

"Oh, yes," I said, looking away. "My timing is impeccable. So does that mean I'm on the auction block?"

"You?" he asked in an incredulous tone. "Of course not. *You*," he said, his gaze traveling over me pointedly, "are priceless. There's no sum I'd agree to part with you for, not now that you're finally mine."

"How charming," I said. "And here I thought I was a few decades too old for you."

He chuckled, his arm draped around the seat behind me. "My brother and I never shared the same tastes. Not where that's concerned."

"So you don't partake, you just facilitate," I said. "Forgive me for seeing a distinction without a difference."

"You're forgiven," he said without missing a beat. "But don't worry. I know how you are. And I must admit, I spent a good deal of time trying to decide what to do with you. Shortly after my brother's death, torturing and then killing you seemed like it would be satisfying enough."

"What changed?" I asked.

He looked at me as if it should be obvious. "There are few things in this world that are off-limits to me, James. Even fewer that have ever posed a challenge, but you... You evaded me so skillfully, and for so long, it was hard not to be impressed. You took from me, and my personal grievances with my brother aside, that's not something I can overlook. But you gave me something in return. And do you know what that is?"

"I can't imagine," I said boredly.

Lewis smiled as he leaned in, close enough that I could feel his breath on my skin. "Obsession. And I'm sure I don't need to tell you this, but for men like us, that's the next best thing to love, isn't it?"

I looked away, trying to mask my irritation. God, he was such a neckbeard. And he kind of sounded like Silas. Was I really so lovestruck that I just hadn't noticed it before?

Chapter 28

"I'm flattered, really," I said. "Would you like an autograph? Because you didn't need to go to all this trouble."

He snorted. "Defiance. Luckily for you, I find it charming," he said, stroking the hair back from my neck. My skin crawled at his touch, but I was sure he had far more than that planned. "I'm going to enjoy breaking you down, bit by bit. We have so much to look forward to."

"I can't wait," I said flatly. "So why did you bring me *here*?"

"To enjoy the show, of course," he said, pulling his arm around me to pull me against his side. I strained away, but he tightened his vice grip, wrapping one hand around my neck and squeezing at just the right spot, just hard enough to compress my jugular until I started to get lightheaded.

"Don't be like that," he scolded. "The fun is about to begin."

I looked down as I saw the first captive being dragged out onto the stage. The young woman was shivering, either from fear or the fact that she was wearing a short red sleeveless gown in a room that was surprisingly chilly for being in a tropical location. Probably both.

The auctioneer began the bidding for her like she was an object, and the bites came in immediately with the man in the front row offering twenty thousand.

"See him?" Lewis asked, pointing to the man who'd started the bidding. "That's Mickey Romero. You've seen him on the nightly news, I assume?" Seeming to take my silence as an answer, he continued, "And that man in the rabbit mask and gray suit over there—that's the new head of operations for the Masdon family of New York. He took over for his predecessor maybe two or three months after you killed him."

I'd been trying to keep my expression neutral, but it was clear from the glee in his eyes that I had failed.

"Oh, I'm sorry," he said in a tone dripping with condescension. "Did you actually think you could accomplish something there? That's precious. But see, that's what I wanted you here for tonight, James. For all your brilliance, you excel at lying to yourself. Thinking you can play vigilante... thinking it would actually accomplish anything. After all the people you killed, including my brother, what have you actually accomplished in reality?"

"Killing your brother was the end, not just the means," I answered.

He chuckled. "Maybe so, but all the others?" he challenged. "You can lie to yourself, but you can't lie to me, James. You are so desperate to give it all meaning. To give your *life* meaning. But you can't. Take that teacher of yours, for example. How many years did you spend at his side?"

"Enough," I said through my teeth.

"And what do you have to show for it?" he taunted. "He tried to kill you in the end, didn't he?"

"As much as I appreciate a good walk down memory lane, is there a point to your little speech?" I asked.

Lewis sneered. "That's just it, love. There isn't one. There is no point to any of this other than what we get out of it. As for what *I* get out of it, well... there's money and power beyond just about anyone's wildest dreams. And now there's you. I'd say that's a pretty good arrangement. You, on the other hand..." He gave a sympathetic tsk. "You're not so fortunate."

Chapter 28

The bidding continued as I tried to keep my expression neutral. Lewis seemed about to say something else when the lights flickered overhead, and the young man who had just been led out onto the stage looked up nervously.

A few seconds later, the lights died completely, and anxious whispers started spreading through the crowd as people tried to figure out whether this was part of the show.

Judging from what I could see of Lewis's face in the shadows, it wasn't.

Interesting.

"I'll be back," he muttered, getting up from his seat. He stopped at the door, and I heard him ordering the young guard to make sure I didn't go anywhere.

I had already isolated the weak link, and now, it seemed, fate had given me the opportunity I had been waiting for.

"It won't be long now," I told the boy as he reentered the box.

I could tell from the way his grip tightened on his gun and his eyes kept darting back and forth between me and the door that I had succeeded at piquing his interest. "What are you talking about?"

"This place has backup generators, I'm sure," I told him, knowing I had to craft my lie carefully. As far as I knew, the lights going out was just an accident, and I couldn't count on Silas or the others having come for me. But I'd still use it to my advantage. "You really think it's an accident that the lights went out, when all these important people just happen to be gathered in the same place?"

His eyes narrowed in suspicion. "It was you?" he asked doubtfully.

"Let's just say I have friends everywhere," I said pointedly. I could tell from the look in his eyes that he believed what I was saying at least enough to be unsure, and once the door of doubt was opened, the rest was easy enough. "In an hour's time, the ashes of this place are going to be crawling with deviants. You came here as a victim, and the way I see it, you can either leave as a hero, or as one of them. If you choose the latter, your options are leaving here in cuffs or in a body bag. The choice is yours."

His eyes widened, and I could see the fear in them, warring with the doubt. A little bit of hope, too, which was probably something the poor kid hadn't had in a long time. Long enough that he had given up on waiting for anyone to come and save him and his sister, and he had decided he was going to have to do the job of saving them both the only way he knew how—by being compliant.

I didn't want to hurt him, but I would if I had to. I could only hope that wasn't the only option.

He glanced out into the lobby, and I could hear the increasingly nervous sounds of the other guards talking amongst themselves.

"They should have been able to get the backup generators on by now," he murmured.

He had a point, but I still wasn't getting my hopes up.

His, on the other hand... my life depended on it.

I had learned a long time ago that manipulation, for all the shit people talked about it, could also be used for good given the right circumstances. Sometimes, especially when you were helpless, it was the only defense you had.

"We're running out of time. You need to make a decision," I told him calmly. "What's your name?"

He hesitated, but he met my eyes. "Ben."

I knew I had him. I wasn't sure if he knew it yet, but I did.

Beneath the guns and the suit, he was just a child soldier, scared and looking for guidance. Still holding out hope that someone would come and save him, even if he knew better.

Hopefully it was a lucky day for us both.

"How do I help you?" he asked warily.

Bingo.

"First things first, is your sister somewhere safe?" I asked.

He nodded. "There's another house on the island. She's there. It's about a mile away from here, though."

"Good," I said. "They're all scrambling right now, so they'll probably have taken everyone they're offering up for auction somewhere they can be contained."

"The holding room," Ben said with a nod. "My friend is guarding it."

"A friend?" I echoed. "Is he trustworthy?"

"I trust him with my life," he answered.

"Do you think between the two of you, you could get the others out of here and over to the house where your sister is in the next twenty minutes?" I asked.

He hesitated. "I... think so, yeah."

"Good," I said. "Because this place isn't going to be standing in thirty. Do you have anything I can use to keep in touch with you?"

He hesitated again before reaching for the radio at his side. "Use this. I'll take Kyle's."

I stashed it in my pocket. "Now move. I take it they actually taught you how to use the gun," I said, nodding to it.

"Yeah," he said, tilting his chin up proudly. "Of course."

"If anyone tries to stop you, or questions you, use it," I told him. "Don't stop to think about it."

He nodded, following me over to the door. "Okay. What about after that?"

"I'll send someone for you and the others," I assured him. "Now, can you get me out of here?"

The kid had no real reason to believe me, other than something that might well have been a coincidence, but I could tell from the look in his eyes that he wanted to. And it was always easy enough to convince someone of something they already wanted to believe. For better or for worse.

He glanced over at the door and hesitated again. "Yeah," he finally said, taking the handcuffs off his belt. "It'll be easier if you wear these."

He waited until I turned to put my hands behind my back and allowed him to cuff them.

Just like that, the balance of power between us had shifted, even if I was once again the one in restraints.

Chapter 28

"Come on," Ben said, nudging me toward the door as he kept the gun on my back. I did my best to look like a prisoner as I walked forward and two of the other guards in the hall stopped to look at us, frowning.

"Where are you taking him?" one demanded.

"Boss wants to move him somewhere more secure until the power's back on," Ben answered. To his credit, he was calm and collected. "Any word on the light situation?"

The other guard relaxed somewhat, shaking his head. "Must've been a breaker. These rich bitches are pissed, though. Hospitality had better keep the drinks coming."

Ben scoffed a derisive laugh and nudged me in the back with the barrel of the gun until I started moving forward again.

As soon as we were out of earshot of the others at the base of a covered stairwell, he whispered, "Sorry."

This kid. He would never have lasted long here, anyway. That was the only thing keeping me from feeling guiltier about putting his neck on the line right now.

"You did good," I told him as he unfastened my cuffs. "I don't suppose you have an extra firearm."

He paused, then reached into his hip holster and offered me his pistol. "You're sure about this, right?" he asked, holding on to it for a moment when I reached to take it.

I looked into his eyes, holding his gaze intently. "You do what I say and you and your sister are going to make it out of this place. Together. I promise you that."

Ben took a deep breath and let go of the gun. "I hope you're right, mister."

That made two of us. "Take care of yourself, and be careful," I told him, watching as he left.

I crept up the stairs and out into the empty hallway, finding a room where I could regroup and wait for Ben to radio that his part of the mission had been a success. There was a lot riding on a naïve kid, but if there was one thing I had working to my advantage, it was that Lewis had created his own little world, and he thought he was fully in control of it.

We were about to find out just how true that really was.

The radio crackled and I heard Ben's voice. "This is Ben. Do you copy?" he asked.

"Copy," I answered.

"We evacuated everyone into the truck," he said, his voice shaky with excitement. "No one even tried to stop us. I heard gunfire, though, further down the island by the shoreline. I think your friends are here."

My own heart started beating a bit faster. So they had come for me, after all. Imagine that.

"Right on schedule," I said, trying to sound nonchalant. "Just get the others the hell out of here, and await further instruction."

"Roger that," he said.

Now the rescue mission was over, and the real fun could begin.

29

LUCA

As we flew over the dark, choppy waters of the Atlantic, I couldn't help but feel a mix of emotions.

Getting onto the island was easier said than done. Everything had to be timed perfectly, but I was still riding the high from successfully bringing Timothy home. Silas had arranged to get us a helicopter, but that required taking out the original pilot, and that night, I learned that flying was one of the many skills in Silas's repertoire.

Malcolm had hardly said a word the entire flight, so I assumed that Silas had read him the riot act. That wasn't stopping him from glowering at me like *I* was the one who'd fucked everything up, but I really didn't give a shit what he thought right now. He could take it up with me later.

The island came into view, and I could see the sprawling mansion that served as the lair of the man who had taken my son. It was surrounded by lush green foliage and a high fence, but we were going to be going in through the rooftop entrance as "employees" now that we'd had the lights cut.

Silas looked almost normal with his long white hair hidden beneath a pilot's cap, and Malcolm, well... he blended in with the other guards I could see prowling around the outside well enough.

I frowned, squinting into the distance. "Is that smoke?"

Silas followed my gaze, his expression turning to one of shock when he saw the gray tendrils billowing up from the sides of the mansion. They were small at first glance, but the closer we drew, the better I could see them.

"Shit, the place is burning down," Malcolm remarked as Silas lowered the helicopter toward the rooftop.

My heart started hammering in my chest. This had James's name written all over it.

"Easy," said Silas. "We haven't even landed yet."

It was only then that I realized I was gripping the handlebar above the helicopter door like I planned on jumping out, sans parachute.

"Right," I muttered. "I'm guessing this place doesn't have a fire department?"

"I'll take out the guards down there," Malcolm said as he prepared to leap out of the open chopper now that it had landed. "You guys are going through the roof."

"That is the plan," said Silas.

Malcolm just rolled his eyes and took off for what I assumed was the fire escape, but knowing him, I wouldn't have been shocked if he planned on rapelling down just for the hell of it.

I got out and ran over to the metal door on the rooftop, not surprised when it refused to budge when I yanked on the handle. After two solid kicks, the door caved in, but it caught against something inside and I heard chains rattling.

Holy shit, whoever had done this really didn't want anyone getting in. Or out.

"I have something in the chopper," Silas said, seemingly oblivious to the gunfire sounding below us. Or he just didn't give a shit.

I froze, wondering how Malcolm was faring. "Should we—?"

"He's fine," Silas said in a nonchalant tone, already digging through the back of the chopper. He came back with a pair of massive bolt cutters and shoved the door open again as far as it would go before slicing through the chains inside. For being as lean as he was, he was surprisingly strong.

There was no smoke coming through the top floor yet, but I could still smell it in the air as we entered the hallway. It was thick enough to make me choke.

"Here," Silas said, offering me one of the bandanas he had taken out of his pocket.

"You really are MacGyver, aren't you?" I asked dryly.

"Former Boy Scout," he said. "It never hurts to be prepared."

I blinked at him. "I can never tell if you're joking."

He just snorted and walked further down the hall, pausing halfway down it. He grew solemn all of a sudden, as if he was listening for something.

"Do you hear that?" he asked.

I was about to say I didn't when I focused and caught the unmistakable sound of screams below. It was a safe bet the other occupants of the building had noticed the fire by now.

"You think this was James, or...?" I asked, keeping my gun drawn and my eyes peeled. As far as I could tell, there was no one else on this floor, but I knew that didn't mean we were guaranteed peace for long.

"It does have James's handiwork on it," Silas answered. "He's always had a flair for the dramatic."

"Yeah," I said with a sigh, trying not to show how fucking scared I was. Not of whoever else we might run into, but of the possibility that James was already...

No, I wasn't going to let myself go there. I couldn't. The thought itself was enough to drive me insane.

I became distinctly aware of Silas watching me as we crept down the hall, checking each room. Most of them were empty, but the fact that this place was set up like some kind of fucked-up hotel for the rich and famous was not lost on me.

When I got my hands on Lewis, I had more than a few bones to pick with him.

Getting James the fuck out of here took priority, though, no matter what he had to say about it. And I was never letting him out of my fucking sight again. He had started out as Silas's prisoner, but now he was mine.

"Come on," I said as Silas hesitated near the stairwell. "We have to keep moving."

He hesitated a bit too long for my liking, so my impatience got the better of me and I headed for the stairwell myself. I had to break down the door since it had been locked as well, but at least it wasn't chained.

I had to keep my thoughts under strict control. If I let them wander too far, I was going to lose my mind. The prospect of losing James was more terrifying than I could handle, so my brain was just shutting down the idea, refusing to allow it to take hold.

"Wait," I said once we came to the bottom of the stairwell and I could hear the direction where the screams were the loudest. "That must be where everyone is being kept."

"It's a theater," Silas murmured, looking around. "I recognize the architecture. That's probably the main hall downstairs, but there should be upper-level seating. Might give us a better view."

I nodded, following him down the hall. Leave it to fucking Silas to know his way around somewhere he had never been before. And of course it was a fucking theater.

"There," Silas said, nodding up ahead. Before I could reach the door, I heard someone shouting down the hall and froze.

A guard came rushing around the corner, but before he could stop us, I fired instinctively. He hit the ground and Silas looked up at me, raising an eyebrow.

"Not bad, DiFiore."

"Whatever," I muttered, annoyed he and Malcolm always acted like I was new to this shit.

Just because I wasn't a hired killer didn't mean I was going to piss myself at the first sign of violence.

Sure as hell not when the man I loved was on the line.

"In here," I said, nodding toward the door to what I assumed was one of the box seats.

Silas nodded and motioned for me to be silent as he slipped in and reappeared a second later to announce that it was all clear. I followed his lead and stayed close to the wall, concealed partially by the curtains wrapped around the box.

As soon as I entered the private seat, the screams billowed out from below, and I could see the teeming crowd trapped in the theater, trampling each other in a desperate bid to escape. While my initial response was to want to help, the fact that every single one of them was an adult wearing some kind of creepy animal mask put that to rest real fast.

I scanned the crowd for any sign of James, or anyone who looked innocent, or like they might be here against their will—but while there were plenty of people panicking as they clawed at each other to get away, there didn't seem to be anyone who fit that criteria.

And I didn't see any sign of James, either, which was at once a relief and a cause for concern.

Where the fuck was he?

And for that matter, where was Lewis?

Chapter 29

Whatever had happened, it was clearly James's doing. It had to be. There was no way Lewis would unleash this kind of chaos on his own property, and with a packed house, no less. Which meant that James had somehow gotten free from his captor.

I wasn't surprised at all. He was nothing if not strong, and too damn smart for anyone's good. I had never thought it was possible to be afraid of someone and admire them so much at the same time.

Right now, though, I was just afraid *for* him.

I was about to give up when I spotted something across the theater. Something in the shadows.

I froze as I stared into the box beside us and realized it was James standing there, staring at me like he was every bit as shocked as I was.

"James?" I murmured, freezing when I saw the shadow behind him.

"Luca?"

"No!" I cried, terrified it was too late.

30

JAMES

"Luca?" I choked out in disbelief, catching sight of the man across the theater.

No. He wasn't supposed to be in here. How did he even—?

Before I could finish that thought, I saw him yelling something to me. Then I felt the gun at my temple and the body at my back.

My spine went rigid as I realized I had let my guard down. Which was exactly what I'd been afraid would happen from the beginning with Luca.

Well, maybe not in the beginning. It had taken the fucker longer than that to worm his way past my defenses, and in that regard, I had sorely underestimated him. He was far more nefarious than I had given him any credit for, and I knew from the way my heart at once sank and leaped at the sight of him here in this place—the last fucking place he was supposed to be, the dumbass—trying to fight it was a lost cause.

Chapter 30

It was still plenty ridiculous that Luca thought he loved me, but as self-destructive as it was, I found myself wondering... did I love him in return?

I didn't think I would be here otherwise, and even now that I was almost certainly about to die, I wouldn't have changed anything.

Except perhaps I would've restrained him, or at least given him something to knock him out for longer so he would be with his son right now rather than trying to fucking rescue me. Goddamn Mafia Waltons.

I felt Lewis's other arm as it wrapped around me from behind, pulling me close enough to him that I was going to need one of those showers they gave people who had been exposed to nuclear hazards, complete with the wire brush and everything.

"There you are," Lewis said, his voice raspy from the smoke. As high as the ceilings in the theater were, it was only a matter of time before it got to us both. "You didn't think I would let you get away that easily, did you?"

"I don't know, you seem perfectly content with the idea that someone like you could get away with everything you have all this time," I said, fairly certain he hadn't yet spotted Luca. Luca had vanished from view, and if he knew what was good for him, he was going to stay gone.

Of course, I knew he wouldn't. He was a DiFiore. It was absolutely delusional to think that he was capable of self-preservation to any degree, but a man could dream.

It was strange how I had spent so many years resenting Silas for abandoning me because I loved him. And now, because I loved Luca, I wanted nothing more than for him to do the same. I wanted him to turn and leave this place, to be with his son, even if it meant I never saw him again.

This was love, wasn't it? It seemed a painful irony that I would figure it out right before I died.

No, actually, that sounded about right.

"Did you really think this was going to work?" Lewis asked bitterly. "Did you really think you could turn it all around and be the hero for once?"

"No," I said boredly. "I've always been perfectly comfortable playing the villain, and I'm good at it. I don't see much point in changing now. But dragging you to hell with me? Now *that* sounds lovely."

He released me only to strike my head with the side of the gun, hard enough to send me sprawling into the railing. My ears rang and my head spun, but I managed to catch myself against the railing, and before I could aim my own weapon, Lewis fired, knocking it out of my grasp.

I hissed as the bullet grazed the meat of my thumb and clutched it instinctively.

Lewis walked toward me, his mouth covered by the back of his hand as he coughed. "You know, I was going to enjoy you for a while longer, but it's quite clear you're not what I thought you were."

"You flatter me," I quipped, watching as Luca appeared in the doorway behind him, raising a finger to his lips.

As if I was just going to blurt out right in front of Lewis, *Luca! There you are! You took your sweet fucking time!*

Chapter 30

My lovable idiot.

Luca pressed the barrel of his gun to the back of the other man's head, and Lewis froze.

"Put the gun down," Luca warned him.

Lewis's eyes burned with spite as he stared at me. For a few moments, I could tell he was trying to decide whether it was worth dying as long as he got to take me out in the process, and if he had been anyone else, I would have been able to respect that.

Eventually, he lowered the gun, and the second he did, I took the opportunity to return the favor, firing a shot into his right forearm and another to his left kneecap.

With a pained groan, Lewis collapsed, clutching his wounds as blood gushed freely from them, and I looked up as Luca rushed into the room.

"Don't kill him," I said as Luca snatched the other man's gun and trained it on him. "I want him alive."

"Would you look at that," Luca muttered, shoving the gun into his waistband and wrapping his thick arm around Lewis's throat to choke him out. "We agree on something."

"You shouldn't be here," I said, watching as Lewis's struggling ceased and the light of consciousness rapidly left his eyes.

"That makes two of us," he said pointedly, getting up once the man was on the floor and Silas came into the room. The lower half of his face was covered like Luca's, but they were both still coughing from the smoke.

So was I, for that matter.

Silas froze, looking between us, then down at Lewis. "Is he—?"

"Not yet," said Luca. "You take him. I've got James."

Before I could protest, Luca had my arm draped over his shoulder and he was leading me out of the box seat.

"I'm fine," I muttered.

"Would you stop being so stubborn for five seconds so we can get out of this place?" Luca growled, tearing the bandana off his face to press it over mine. "Wear this."

I was admittedly a bit dizzy, so I took it. "How did you even get here?" I asked through the fabric, resisting the urge to breathe in his scent. I'd missed him more than I wanted to admit.

"That's a long story," Luca said in between coughs. "But I'm more interested in getting the fuck out of here before the place burns down."

"I hadn't really planned on getting out," I admitted, feeling the scathing look he was giving me. I was sure the thickening smoke was the only reason I wasn't getting a lecture right now, but I was so relieved to see him, I didn't give a shit.

Relieved. Enraged. I was used to contradictory emotions where Luca was concerned.

I was never going to be able to lay claim to being a rational man again, but I was surprisingly okay with that.

As soon as we were outside on the rooftop, Luca turned to me and took my face in his hands. I wasn't used to seeing concern in someone's eyes when they looked at me.

Chapter 30

Certainly not someone like him, and yet, there was no room to doubt it was genuine.

"Are you okay?" he demanded. He brushed his thumb over what I was sure was a bruise forming over my eye where Lewis had struck me with his gun, and it stung like a bitch. It still felt so good to be touched by Luca, though.

"I'm fine," I said, and for once, I meant it. Everything fucking hurt, and my lungs felt like I had just spent a few hours at Chernobyl, but Luca was here, alive and with me. That was more than I had any right to ask for. It was more than I had ever allowed myself to want. "What about Timothy?"

Luca frowned, staring at me for a few moments with an unreadable expression. "Timothy is fine. He was at the drop site, right where we expected."

"I know," I said, leaning against the side of the chopper. "But you should be with him, not here."

"I'll keep that in mind," Luca said dryly.

Silas was already on the rooftop, dragging Lewis out of the theater, but just because he was preoccupied didn't mean he was going to be distracted forever.

"I don't mean to question your rescue mission, but did you have to bring him?" I asked.

"Wait till you find out Malcolm is here," Luca said.

I grimaced. "Wonderful."

"I'm not going to let anyone touch you, James," Lucas said, holding my gaze. "That should be obvious by now, but in case it isn't, let me make it abundantly clear. You're mine, and you're not going anywhere. No one is taking you from me again. Not even you yourself."

I stared at him in silence for a few moments, biting back the impulse to argue even when I really didn't want to.

"Yours?" I echoed. "Is that an agreement you came to with Silas, or are you just winging it?"

"Pretty much winging it at this point," he admitted. "How am I doing so far?"

His hand traveled down to rest against my cheek, gently stroking the bruised flesh.

My throat tightened for some reason. Probably just the smoke. "Decently," I told him. "This whole domineering mob boss thing looks good on you."

"Oh, yeah?" There was a mischievous glint in his eyes as he took a step closer, leaning in to press his lips against mine. "Maybe you can help me practice," he murmured into the kiss.

My lips parted instinctively, and I found myself entangled in a kiss more intimate and passionate than any of the ones we had shared so far.

This time, it was relief rather than hatred fanning the flames, but I wasn't complaining. Everything was more intense when it came to Luca. It didn't matter how positive or negative the emotion was. He made me feel things that no one else ever had. Even things I had once thought I understood, like love and obsession, seemed so pale in comparison to what he stirred within me.

"You came for me," I said quietly.

Chapter 30

Luca frowned, as if he didn't understand. "Of course I did," he muttered. "I meant what I said, James. I love you."

I frowned. Those words made less sense now than ever. "I thought that was some sort of reverse Stockholm syndrome thing that would wear off when you got your son back."

Luca gave me a withering glare that was somehow affectionate. "Yeah, well, I guess you're wrong," he said flatly. "Imagine that."

"I suppose it's nice to be wrong sometimes," I admitted. "First time for everything."

Luca's lips quirked at one end. "You get used to it eventually. You don't really have a choice."

"So, does that make me your prisoner now?" I asked.

Luca paused to consider it. "Yeah, I guess it does," he answered. "You got a problem with that?"

I slipped my arms around his neck and ran my fingers through his hair. I found myself wanting to keep touching him, just to remind myself he was real. To remind myself he was really here. We both were.

"No," I said with a sigh. "I can't say I do."

Luca kissed me again, and I found myself melting against him, not wanting this to stop anytime soon.

Of course, Silas cleared his throat, an unwelcome reminder of the fact that he was, in fact, still here.

"We're going to need to discuss this," he said, looking from me to Luca.

Luca held his gaze unapologetically. "We can discuss it all you like," he said with a shrug. "But that's how it's going to be."

Silas was tense like he was about to argue, but he just sighed. "We'll table the matter until we get back. This is going to be the cleanup of the century."

"There's a house on the other side of the island," I said, meeting Silas's gaze. "Two of the younger guards defected on Lewis and evacuated his captives. Make sure they're not harmed." I clenched my jaw to eke out the word lagging behind the others. "Please."

Silas watched me for a moment, his expression unreadable, before nodding. He looked back at the theater. "I'm not in any hurry to call the fire department," he said flatly. "I think this can resolve itself."

"It's not over," I said through my teeth, looking up at Luca. "There are others. This island is just one part of Lewis's operations."

"A huge part that's over now," Luca replied. "Because of you. Now, come on. Let's go home."

Home.

For some reason, that word affected me more than it probably should have. It filled me with a strange sense of peace. Belonging.

That was new.

Luca was full of surprises, and when I was with him, so was I.

"Yes," I said, taking his hand. "Let's go home."

31

LUCA

The next twelve hours were a fucking blur. Not that I had been living on normal time for a while now. When it came to any involvement in Silas and Malcolm's bullshit, there was always the factor of a time warp that had to be considered.

And then there was James.

James, A.K.A. Chris, the man who had deceived my brother and the rest of our family for years, A.K.A. Demon, the infamous serial killer who had brought no shortage of chaos into my life.

James, the man who had given himself over to protect me and mine for no reason other than the same reason he did everything else—because he wanted to.

And apparently, what he wanted was me.

And what I wanted was him.

That was the one thing we had in common. It was the one overriding factor to all the myriad reasons why this thing between us made no sense, was incredibly self-destructive on both our parts, and really just shouldn't have been capable of happening in a logical world.

And yet, as I stared at him across the living room, trying to be patient about the fact that Silas was monopolizing him in the interest of debriefing him on everything that had just happened—and thus pushing my goal of debriefing him in an entirely different way even further out—I didn't care.

I didn't want to live in my sane, rational world anymore. The world I had clung to so hard while my family seemed to be trying to drag me out of it, kicking and screaming.

And now, I wanted to live in his world instead, even though it was a swirling, chaotic void of violence and mayhem. It wasn't because I actually craved any of those things, but because I craved him, and that was the world he lived in.

Because I needed him.

And I was willing not only to go to hell and back, but also to set up a nice little house there with a white picket fence and everything as long as it meant keeping him.

As much as I just wanted to be alone with him right now, and tell him all those things and more—all the things I wasn't sure I was ever going to get a chance to say, rather than them haunting me like ghosts for the rest of my life—I kept my mouth shut.

We were going to be fighting an uphill battle when it came to convincing Silas, let alone Malcolm, that James belonged at my side and not in an underground prison, even after everything that had happened.

Chapter 31

The logical part of my brain understood where they were coming from, but there was nothing logical about my feelings for James, and I had given up trying to force them to conform to anything resembling reason a long damn time ago.

Sanity was overrated, anyway.

When James finally finished recounting all the details of his expedition, I was even more impressed—and nauseated by the thought of what had nearly happened to him.

What he had put on the line for me, and for my son.

"This is a lot to take in," Enzo said, rubbing his eyes. He had been asleep when we got in, and I knew he had only gone to bed to get a couple of hours of shut eye once we were safely leaving the island.

How he and Val handled all the shit Silas and Malcolm got up to without developing a drinking problem was beyond me. I was already working out my contingency plans if this thing went sideways and they tried to take James away from me.

Plan A was convincing them, but plan B was running away with James and Timothy, which was going to come with a host of problems on its own. A host of problems that were entirely preferable to the idea of living without him, of not protecting him, whether he wanted me to or not.

"Indeed, it is," Silas said, seated next to his husband. He was always watching Enzo protectively, every second of every day, and while my brother was perfectly formidable in his own right, it was something I understood now better than I ever had.

It didn't matter how strong James was. It didn't matter how capable he was, or how much shit he had already survived. I didn't want him to have to do it on his own. I didn't want him to have to fend for himself, and as long as I was still taking breaths, he wasn't going to. Never again.

"I'm just glad you guys are all okay. And that you got all the captives out," said Valentine, who had remained dead silent while James spoke. Even I hadn't known what to say, torn between retroactive dread over everything that had happened to James and relief that he was still with us. Still with me.

"What's going to happen to them now?" Enzo asked, looking over at his husband.

"The appropriate channels have been notified," Silas answered. "They're safe now, and once they're all checked out and given the care and attention they need, the ones who are young enough will be moved into qualified foster homes, where they can hopefully begin to start healing from all the horrors they've had to endure."

My stomach churned if I even thought about it, and as a father, it was too horrible to do that without losing my mind. Nothing was ever going to make what those kids had been through at the hands of the Capello family okay, but they were free now, and that was a start.

Thanks to James.

"There's gotta be something we can do," said Enzo. "Some way we can help."

"We'll do whatever we can, love," Silas said, putting a hand on his shoulder. "Right now, they're safe with good people. But we still have some things to work out."

I could feel the others' attention shift back to James, and I immediately grew defensive.

I understood why they were wary of him. I did. He had put his own neck on the line for me and my son, and he'd saved all those kids, but he was still Demon. He was still unpredictable, brilliant, and capable of things most people couldn't even fathom.

But he was also mine, and that was the variable I wasn't sure they were counting on.

I picked my battles in this family—it was a matter of keeping my own sanity as much as anything—but this was one battle I was never going to lose, and if they pushed me, they were going to find out the hard way.

"Am I the only one who has any damn common sense left?" Malcolm asked in his usual gruff way. "Do I need to point out the obvious, that no matter what he did, he's still a serial killer? He's still fucking Demon, and we've got him sitting on our couch wearing a fucking Sherpa blanket like he's some lost and wounded soul who was just in the wrong place at the wrong time?"

"Would you prefer if it was fleece?" Enzo quipped before I had the chance to say anything. It was probably just to ease some of the tension and keep it from devolving into a fight between me and Malcolm, which was pretty much inevitable, but I appreciated it all the same.

Malcolm just glared at him, which in turn made Silas seethe.

"I'm just saying, it's bullshit," Malcolm growled. "And it's time we talked about what to do before this gets out of hand."

"It already got out of hand," I said through my teeth. "We did things your way, and it almost got us all killed, my kid included. You're fucking lucky I don't want your head, even if it's only for Val's sake."

Malcolm snorted. "I offered you an opportunity, and you took it."

"Yeah, I did," I agreed. "And it was a mistake. It's not one I'm going to make again, so if you want to put him back in a cell, you're going to have to put me in it, too."

"Luca," James said, staring at me nervously. "I appreciate what you're trying to do, but—"

"No," I snapped. "No, I'm sick of the double standards in this family. I'm sick of these two twisted motherfuckers pretending like you're the problem and they're not. And I'm sick of Malcolm acting like you're the devil, when that's literally his goddamn moniker, and Owen was some saint because he doesn't know the truth."

Malcolm was up from his seat immediately, giving me a murderous glare I knew well. Before, it would've made me back down, but when it came to James—when it came to protecting who I loved—I was fearless. There was nothing I could possibly lose that mattered more than my family. And now, he was a part of that.

A part of me.

"You'd better watch your mouth and stop talking shit about things you know nothing about," Malcolm snarled as Valentine grabbed his arm to hold him back. Even Silas looked like he was ready to intervene when I didn't back down.

"I do know. More than you," I said firmly. "I'm not saying Owen deserved what happened, and I'm not saying what James did was remotely okay, but he's never killed an innocent person, and that's a hell of a lot more than I can say for Owen."

"You son of a—"

Valentine pushed against Malcolm's chest before he could lunge, and Malcolm froze, but even though I knew he wasn't willing to risk hurting his husband, I could still see the venom in his eyes. The rage.

"Be careful, Luca," Silas said in a warning tone. "Be careful what you're saying. I know you're emotional right now. We all are, but—"

I scoffed. Silas, emotional? Yeah, that was a laugh. Maybe where Enzo was concerned. But I wasn't going to back down. "It's the truth," I said, looking over at James, who had a neutral expression even though I could see he was ready to intervene, too.

Ready to come to my defense, even if it meant the others would turn on him. Malcolm would shoot him right between the eyes at the slightest provocation. Anything to give him an excuse to do what he'd always wanted to.

I just wasn't going to let that happen.

"What are you saying?" Enzo asked warily. Silas was listening, too, and for the moment, so was Malcolm, even if it was only because he was trying in vain to calm down like a fucking bull in a china shop.

"Exactly what I said," I answered with a shrug. "Owen killed someone. It wasn't premeditated, but there's still a dead girl's family out there who's never going to get to see her graduate high school or college, or get married or have kids, or anything else because of him—all because he wanted to have some fun at a party and drive home drunk, and because his rich daddy was important enough to make sure he didn't face the consequences. That girl never got justice. At least not in any official capacity."

"You're lying," Malcolm seethed, shirking out of Valentine's grasp. I could see the doubt in his eyes, though. Whether he wanted to admit it or not, he knew his husband wasn't innocent. It was the kind of truth that was just easier to gloss over in the interest of not speaking ill of the dead, but like me with my first marriage, there had to be a part of him that knew everything wasn't as perfect as it had seemed.

A part of him that knew he was making a saint out of the person he loved, because I could tell that even though this revelation came as a shock, he wasn't sure. He was afraid it was true, and more than anything, that was why he was so furious.

"I'm not lying. But you don't need to take my word for it. The records were sealed, but I'm sure you and Silas have both dug up skeletons buried deeper than that," I said pointedly. "You just didn't want to. Not when it came to him."

For a few moments, Malcolm said nothing, and I was sure he was going to snap at any second. Valentine's hand on his shoulder seemed to calm him down a little more, though, and I could see the doubt setting in.

Malcolm finally turned to Silas. "Is that true?" he demanded.

Silas hesitated. "I don't... I don't know. There was something in his file that was sealed when I looked into him years back, so it's possible. I just didn't see a reason to dig any further."

I could see the dread in Malcolm's eyes as reality and his own memories began to diverge. And in a way, I could sympathize with him. If anyone else were in the middle of this, we probably wouldn't be on opposing sides, but just as he felt the duty to protect those he loved and had sworn to protect, I had to do the same.

"Even if it's true, it didn't give you the right to do what you did," he said in a dangerously quiet tone, turning his furious glare on James.

"No," James said to my surprise. "It didn't. There are many things I've done that I didn't have the right to do, and this may not mean anything to you, but I regret what I did to Owen. He fit my code, but that's only because I bent my rules. Because I wanted to hurt Silas, and the best way—the *only* way—I could do that was through you. And for that, I am sorry. I know it doesn't mean anything, and I don't expect you to believe me... but I am."

Fresh anger glowed in Malcolm's eyes, and I prepared myself to fight, already moving to get between them.

Silas, who had been listening in silence until then, seemed similarly wary. He was poised to intervene, too.

Malcolm continued to stare James down, at least as much as he could when I was acting as a human shield in front of him. He finally relaxed his posture slightly, but his jaw was still clenched.

"I don't accept your fucking apology. And if it were up to me, you'd be dead," he said, his voice unnervingly calm and gravelly, which I knew was an even bigger warning sign than his anger and outbursts.

Malcolm's gaze finally traveled over to me. "But if you want to spend the rest of your life playing warden to this fucking psycho, so be it. Just don't come crying to me when he chops you up in your sleep."

With that, he stood and left the room.

Valentine froze for a moment, looking over at me and James. "He just needs time," he said carefully.

"Yeah." I sighed. "About a millennium should do it."

Valentine gave me an apologetic glance before going after his husband. Only he was capable of calming Malcolm down, and my personal feelings aside, I couldn't really say I blamed the guy.

"I suppose that puts the ball in my court," Silas said with a heavy sigh.

No matter what he thought, I wasn't letting him take James from me, but for the moment, I decided to let cooler heads prevail and kept my mouth shut to see what side he was going to come down on. Just because I was in fight or flight mode—the only two instincts I seemed to know at this point—that didn't mean I had to get stupid.

Although I was starting to understand Malcolm's caveman impulses better than I ever had before.

Chapter 31

"James can't be allowed to roam freely," Silas began in that condescending tone that was begging for an ass kicking. Even if I was almost certainly going to die in the process. "That said, if you're willing to take on responsibility for him, I don't see why the current arrangement can't continue on a trial basis. If he proves himself perfectly trustworthy, then we can talk about removing the collar. Until then, we'll give him a less lethal one."

"Proves himself? He put his life on the line to rescue my kid," I protested. "He could've left me for dead at the docks and had his freedom if that's what he wanted, but he didn't. He came back for me, and he's had a thousand other chances to betray me since then, but he hasn't."

"That may be so, but he has tried to kill fifty percent of the people in this house," Silas said dryly.

I gritted my teeth. He had a point whether I wanted to admit it or not. I knew I wasn't being logical, but the urge to defend James was strong to say the least.

"That's fair," said James. "And for what it's worth, I apologize for most of those attempted murders. Not yours, though. *You* had it coming."

Silas stared blankly at him. "Your partial apology is noted."

"If it makes you feel better, I'm not obsessed with you anymore," James continued. "As it turns out, you were a shitty boyfriend, an even worse teacher, and when it comes to being a lover..." He grimaced. "As far as I'm concerned, we can just chalk the whole thing up to a sampling error, because quite frankly, I had even less of a social life then than I did in your underground prison, and I really didn't have all that much to compare you to."

Silas narrowed his eyes. "I'm not going to dignify that with a response."

"Different strokes for different folks," Enzo said, putting a hand on his husband's shoulder. There was a gleam in his eyes. "I've got no complaints."

"Points for self-improvement, I suppose," James said with a dismissive shrug, earning another glare from Silas. "My point is, I'm fine with wearing the collar. I don't care about proving myself to any of you, but you're Luca's family and he prefers you alive, so it is what it is."

"Touching," Enzo said flatly. "Actually, I think you'll fit right in here."

"There is one more condition," said Silas. "I think it would be best if you two and Timothy stayed here for a period of one year. Then we can revisit this. Just so I can keep an eye on you all, and make sure there aren't going to be any..." He paused to choose his words carefully. "Relapses."

"You want us to live here? In the same fucking house?" I asked in disbelief.

"It'll be just like old times," Enzo said, sounding way too into it. And the worst part was, I knew Valentine was going to be even more giddy about the idea.

"How cozy," James said flatly. "I don't suppose the underground prison is still an option?"

I sighed. "One year," I said firmly. "That's all."

"And then we revisit," Silas countered. "Think of it as giving Timothy more quality time with his family."

"You mean more time for you guys to indoctrinate him into the family business bullshit," I argued.

"You've always had one foot in and one foot out," said Enzo. "But now, you guys are together. And before you look at me like that, it's not a dig. I'm just stating facts. You're going to have to accept the fact that living a normal life wasn't ever a possibility for any of us, Luca. You're a DiFiore, same as the rest of us. And so is Timothy. The way I see it, you can either embrace that, and we can all actually start acting like a family for once and be stronger for it, or we can be vulnerable, living our separate lives and trying to fight it."

"The hair gel model does make a decent point," James mused. "When I was trying to kill you all, it was easy to exploit the separation. For God's sake, you didn't even notice I was your brother-in-law's boss," he said, turning to Silas. "Talk about forgetting to cross your T's and dot your I's."

"Oh, it's going to be so much fun having you around the house," Silas said in a wry tone.

James just gave him an innocent smile. It clearly went right up Silas's ass, but I found it charming.

Yeah, Malcolm was right about one thing. I was in deep.

I heard something moving by the stairs and looked up, tensing as I expected it to be Malcolm having second thoughts about his decision to grudgingly form a truce. I was relieved to see Timothy standing at the top of the stairs, rubbing his eyes.

"Daddy?" He yawned.

"Hey, kiddo," I said, walking over to lift him into my arms. I kissed his forehead before carrying him back over to the couch with me.

James tensed up as if I had just walked over with a loaded nuclear warhead.

"Who's that?" Timothy asked, looking over my shoulder at James with a curious gaze.

"This is James, buddy," I answered, deciding to just go with the simplest, most direct approach. I wasn't sure exactly what James was going to be comfortable with when it came to his role in Timothy's life, but he and Timothy were the two most important people in my life now, and we had time to figure it out. "He's the one who helped me find you."

Timothy's eyes widened slightly. There was still a lot about everything that had happened that he didn't understand, and for that, I was grateful. The shrink I'd had come out to talk with him while we were rescuing James had confirmed that much. As far as she could tell, he didn't seem to be traumatized by what had happened, just confused, and at least Lewis had kept his word about that. Explaining everything to my in-laws was another matter, but Malcolm had actually proved himself useful in handling the police, so that was one less thing I had to worry about.

I knew as Timothy got older, there were going to be questions that weren't so easy to sweep under the rug. Things he was going to understand that he just didn't have the capacity for now, including who and what James was to me. Things we were just going to have to take one day at a time.

"You're a good guy?" Timothy asked, suddenly wide awake as he stared at James with great interest.

James gave a nervous laugh. I had never seen him like this before. He was more wary around a child than he had been around a man with a gun to his head, and it was kind of adorable. "I wouldn't go that far," he said carefully. "But I have my moments. It's nice to meet you, Timothy. Your daddy talks about you all the time, and I can see why he's so proud. You're a very brave boy."

Timothy grinned from ear to ear. "Uncle Val lets me watch scary movies, and I'm not scared at all."

"He does, does he?" I asked dryly. "We're going to have to have a talk about that."

"In his defense, Val's idea of a scary movie is subjective," Enzo said with a snort.

James chuckled. "That's impressive. I enjoy scary movies myself from time to time."

No surprise there. "Come on, sport," I said, lifting Timothy into my arms again. "It's past your bedtime, and we've all had a long day, so I think everyone should get some sleep."

"Okay," Timmy said, yawning again as he rested his head on my shoulder. "Can you and James read me a bedtime story?"

I looked over at James, who was frozen like a deer in headlights, waiting for me to respond.

"If he wants to," I said.

Timothy looked expectantly at James, who nodded. "All right," James said stiffly. "That sounds... nice."

"Sweet dreams, squirt," Enzo said, walking with Silas down the hall. "See you guys in the morning." He gave me a knowing look.

I rolled my eyes. I knew I was never going to hear the end of it from my brothers. Not only was I with another man after a lifetime of being straight, I was with a serial killer. Debatably the worst out of the bunch of psychos our family seemed to attract like flies to honey.

And yet, there was so much more to him than that. More than the others could see. Only I had ever gotten to see the vulnerable side of him in its entirety, and somehow, that made it even more precious to me.

I, Luca DiFiore, was in love with a monster.

That much was irrefutable. And I knew better than to think I had tamed the savage beast. If anything, I had become one myself, and while James had always been a vigilante acting out his own vendettas, I was something a hell of a lot worse.

I had become a monster not out of any sense of moral judgment or because I had an ax to grind. I had become a monster for love, and if there was one thing Silas and Malcolm had taught me, it was that those monsters were the most dangerous kind of all.

As I headed down the hall to tuck Timothy in, James followed me. He leaned against the wall by the bed, looking around at all the toys and books lining the shelves around the room. Standing next to the mural depicting dinosaurs riding trains that spanned one end of the room to the other, James definitely looked like he was out of his element, which put him in my shoes for once.

"All right, how about this one?" I asked, picking up the *Beauty and the Beast* picture book sitting on the bedside table. I flipped open to the page where I'd last left off.

Chapter 31

It seemed like so long ago now, and for a while, I had thought that might end up being the last story I ever got to tell my son. No matter how exhausted I was, from now on, I was never going to take these moments for granted. I smiled as I watched his eyelids droop to the cadence of my voice until he was fast asleep with only a few paragraphs left to go.

I carefully set the book down on the table and crept out of the room with James following close behind me. I shut the door softly.

We both waited until we were in my bedroom across the hall before either of us spoke. As soon as I shut the door and turned to him, James smirked at me. "That's not the way I recall that story ending."

I raised an eyebrow. "No? What version did you read?"

"The one with jealous, ugly sisters who kept the girl locked up with the beast in hopes he would eat her alive. Proof against the concept of family reunions," he remarked.

I blinked. "Yeah, I can see why that part didn't make it into the kids' version."

"It's open to interpretation, I suppose," James mused.

I pushed him up against the wall, smiling. "You don't seem like the fairy tale type."

"I resent that," James said in a dry tone. "I'll have you know I can be whimsical when I want to be."

"Is that so?" I asked, chuckling as I ran my hands down his lean torso. As much as I wanted to jump his bones, the myriad of cuts and bruises all over his body kept me at bay. For now. "What's your favorite?"

He paused, considering it carefully. "*The Little Mermaid*."

"*The Little Mermaid*?" I echoed, surprised. "Seriously?"

"She turns into seafoam in the end," he answered. "A dramatic exit, if ever there was one. All because she didn't play it safe and listen to her father. You of all people should appreciate that moral."

"Recent events have led me to the conclusion that playing it safe may be overrated," I admitted. "And you're going to be on probation from selecting bedtime stories for a while, FYI."

He blew a puff of air through his nostrils. "You really want me around your son?" he asked, growing serious. "You know who I am. What I'm capable of."

"Yeah, I do," I said. "But that's why. I'm not going to force you into anything you're not ready for, James. I don't think that would be fair to you or Timothy. But I meant what I said before. I love you, and I'm willing to do whatever it takes to make this work."

"You still haven't changed your mind about that?" he asked, frowning doubtfully.

"Nope," I said, holding his gaze.

He drew his bottom lip into his mouth, worrying at it. "I meant what I said, too. If we found our way back to each other..."

I paused to remember what he was talking about. "You're saying you love me, too?"

He nodded, and there was something about the look in his eyes that made my heart ache. Something raw and vulnerable. Like he was afraid of allowing himself to get hurt. And after everything he'd been through, I could understand why.

I hadn't expected him to say it at all, but I knew he did. His actions left little room to doubt it. It was okay with me if he never said the words. He didn't need to.

"I do love you, Luca," he said quietly, and it meant that much more. "But that's always been more of a curse than anything."

"I'm not Silas, James," I said, pressing my hand against his cheek, reveling in the sensation of his warm skin against mine. It was a welcome reminder that he was still here. Still with me. And I wasn't going to let him go.

Ever.

He searched my eyes. "No," he said quietly. "You aren't. But are you sure you know what you're getting into? I have more enemies than just Lewis. And in case you haven't figured it out, I'm crazy. I'm a mess."

"Oh, no doubt there," I agreed, stroking his hair away from his face. "But you're my kind of crazy. And in case you haven't noticed, I'm a mess, too. But the thing is, my crazy likes your crazy, and Enzo is right about one thing—normal was never an option for any of us. But together, as a family, we can be something even better. And you are part of the family now, James, whether you like it or not."

His lips quirked like he was trying not to smile. "Is that so?" he asked. "No opting out?"

"Nope. None whatsoever. You can think of yourself as a captive if you need to," I said, pressing my lips to his.

"And if I want to think of myself as something else?" he asked, his fingers slipping into my hair as he pulled me closer for another kiss. "What might I call that?"

I stopped to think about it, finding that the reservations I probably should have had about putting any official title to my relationship with another man were more molehills than mountains. And they were already crumbling away.

"Boyfriend is probably a good place to start," I answered. "As long as you're good with that."

"I'm good," James said breathlessly, his lips parting to allow my tongue entrance. "Well... you know what I mean."

I laughed, deepening the kiss as I pushed him against the wall. "You're good for me, and maybe I'm a little bad for you. That's all that really matters."

"I like the sound of that," James said, his hands slipping up beneath my shirt. He moaned as my tongue delved deep into his mouth once more, but when my fingertips brushed over the bandages on his right hand, common sense came back to me.

"You're hurt," I said with a ragged sigh against his lips.

He gave me a look. "Just because I fell in love with you doesn't make me some kind of pussy now. Or are you put off by a little blood?"

I gave him a look, dragging him over to the bed. "Okay, tough guy, you asked for it," I said, climbing on top of him.

The light of amusement and mischief in his eyes only spurred on my lust, but I still tried to be careful as I slowly undressed him, fighting back the urge to tear into him like a Christmas present.

Fuck, he was hot. Every inch of his skin I uncovered and touched left me yearning for more, and the sounds of the moans my touch was capable of eliciting from him were music to my ears.

I tugged his pants off, freeing his cock, and while he parted his legs in preparation for me to take him, I found myself intrigued by another part of him I wanted to explore.

Sucking a guy off was about as gay as it got, but there was no hesitation on my part as I took his cock in my hand and sealed my lips around the glistening crown.

"Luca," James gasped in surprise, his hips arching a little off the bed.

I pinned them with my other hand and took him in deeper until half his shaft was resting on my tongue.

He tasted good. Better than good.

I sucked harder, and he moaned, which made me want it even more. I wanted all of him. It didn't matter if I had never wanted another man the way I wanted him. I had never wanted anyone else this way, and the novelty just made it all the more exciting.

"Oh, fuck, Luca," he breathed as I let his cock slide out of my mouth just enough to run my tongue up along the underside of it, still keeping the base firmly in my grip.

I could tell he was getting close, so I stopped what I was doing and took my fingers into my mouth to get them wet. I slipped both digits between his cheeks and started stroking his tight hole in small circles.

A shudder ran up his spine, and I could tell he was trying not to squirm too much as I took him back into my mouth and continued sucking him off as I fingered him, driving into his spot.

His tight hole clenching down around me made me even harder, and it was all I could do not to just jerk myself off. He was so fucking hot. Everything, from the way he moved and squirmed to the way he gasped my name, was like some perfectly tailored spell to keep me enraptured. To keep me wanting more.

"Luca, I'm close. If you don't stop, I'll—"

That was all the confirmation I needed to suck him even harder. He gave another startled gasp, his hips surging off the bed as he dug his fingers into the blankets on either side of them. "Luca!" he cried, his hips bucking wildly.

I couldn't resist the urge to swallow as he came. To taste him.

It was even better than I'd imagined.

I found myself licking his cock clean of the evidence as he collapsed on the bed, breathing raggedly. I spread his cheeks open wider, getting him even wetter with what was left of his come on my tongue and my own saliva.

Seeing him come undone like this for me was too fucking good.

Chapter 31

I stopped to push open his legs, spreading them further apart. My cock was already pulsing with need as I rested it against his entrance. His hole was still slightly agape from my fingers, and I was leaking enough precome to prepare him the rest of the way. Reaching for the bottle of lube somewhere in the bedside table seemed like an insurmountable journey when I needed to be inside him right fucking now. The way he was squirming and clawing at me to pull me closer confirmed he felt the same way.

"Yes," he panted, his nails digging into my shoulders hard enough to draw blood. Fuck, even that felt good. It sent a surge of heat to my cock, and I already felt like I was going to explode as I eased myself inside him. It took all my willpower to be gentle. "Fuck me. Now."

His words—and the desperation behind them—unglued me. Not only was this man capable of awakening a side of me I hadn't even known existed, but he was more than capable of taking it.

I kissed him harder, making him taste his own come, and our tongues tangled messily as I fucked him. My hands were groping every inch of his body they could claim at once, but it still wasn't enough.

And it never would be.

I wanted him too much, too aggressively, too violently, for that hunger to ever be fully sated. But there was a certain satisfaction that came in wanting someone—in wanting the right person, and the wrong one.

And sometimes, that person was both at the same time.

"I love you, James," I whispered against his lips as I fucked him harder, my thrusts quickening. "I love you so much, it fucking scares me."

"It probably should," he breathed. "It's not a great sign for your sanity. Or your morality. Or your sense of self-preservation."

"Probably not," I agreed, raking my hand through his damp hair and pulling his head back to reveal his throat, running my tongue up alongside it. "But I love you all the same."

"Maybe you are the dumb brother," he said wryly, but there was lust mingled with unmistakable love in his eyes.

I smiled against his lips and pinned his good hand against the bed, exploring his body with my other one as I forced myself to slow down, savoring the sensations of being buried inside him—his body pressed to mine, safe in my arms. Mine.

"I can live with that, as long as I'm the one who has you," I replied.

"You're so corny," James muttered.

"You like it," I accused.

His only defense was a strangled moan as I drove directly into his prostate again, feeling myself on the brink of coming. And judging from how stiff his cock was as it rubbed between our bodies with each thrust, he was close again, too.

I drove into him one last time and reached down to take his cock in my hand, giving it a gentle stroke to make sure we climaxed together.

"Luca," James moaned into another kiss, and I slowed my thrusts as my last streams of come pulsed into him.

"Fuck," he panted, staring up at me as we both caught our breath. "What was that?"

"That was how we can spend every night for the rest of our lives, if you agree to it," I told him, gazing down at him.

"Every night, hmm?" he asked with a mischievous but hopeful glimmer in his eyes. "You think you have that much endurance?"

"You said it yourself, I'm not bad for someone who's never been with another guy," I quipped. "But I'm willing to put in the practice, and something tells me you'd make an excellent teacher."

He moaned blissfully, squirming against me as I kissed him again. "Well, I was decent enough at being a doctor and a serial killer. What's one more career change?"

I smiled against his lips. "Yeah, you're a Jack of all trades."

"Jack," he mused. "That does have a certain ring to it."

"Oh, no," I said, carefully pulling out of him before I gathered him into my arms. "Demon is retiring, not rebranding."

"Is that so?" he asked, a spark of challenge in his gaze.

I gave him a look. "You did what you set out to do, James," I murmured. "And the world is a better place as a result of it. But I almost lost you in the process. That's not a risk I'm willing to take ever again."

The defiance in his eyes slowly melted away and he turned from me with a sigh. "There they are. The DiFiore puppy eyes."

I smirked. "Is it working?"

"You know it's working," he mumbled. "But you're wrong. I didn't finish what I set out to do. There's still one loose end."

I listened thoughtfully, piecing his words together. "Lewis."

"He has information," James said, growing somber. "Information we could use to take down others like him."

I listened to what he was saying, and as much as it went against my instincts to keep him here, and keep him safe—which meant keeping him out of trouble—he had a point.

All those people were free and safe because of James, but there were still others out there. Monsters who preyed on the innocent, and the only people who stood a chance at bringing them to justice were monsters of a different kind.

I had my son, and the man I loved, but there were so many others out there who weren't that fortunate.

"I did promise you I would help you take him down when all this was said and done," I said with a sigh.

"You did," said James. "And you don't owe me anything. You did what you promised, and there is a part of me that would love nothing more than to just live your happy, normal, quiet life with you. Not as Demon, but as James—whoever the hell that even is. You're worth figuring it out for. But..."

"But you don't like loose ends," I said quietly.

The look in his eyes was my answer.

Chapter 31

"I've done a lot of things I regret, Luca," he finally said. "But I can live with that. It would be harder to live with knowing I had the chance to do something—something that would actually matter—and giving it up." He looked away. "But I would. For you. For Timothy. If that's what you need, if that's what it takes to be with you, then I'll retire. Demon dies, and James figures out a way to live with that."

I stared at him for a moment, shocked by his words. Shocked by what he was willing to give up for me.

And there was a part of me that wanted to take him up on it. It wasn't the right thing, but it was the safe thing, and I had never in a million years imagined that James would be the angel on my shoulder—even if he was also the demon in my bed—but here we were.

"One last time," I said, looking down at him. "Think of it as a farewell tour," I added when I saw the confusion in his eyes. "We get what we can out of Lewis, and we take out all the names in his little black book, but the operative word here is *we*. You, me, and Silas. Not you going off on your own. And you're not the hired gun on this. You're the mastermind. Those are my conditions."

James's eyes widened slightly as I spoke, something like amusement shining in them. "Conditions," he echoed. "Now you're starting to sound like the villain."

"How am I doing?" I teased.

"Your delivery isn't bad, but we could work on your presentation," he said, pulling me in for another kiss. "I'll agree to your conditions, but I have one of my own."

"Oh, yeah?" I asked, raising an eyebrow. "And what's that?"

"You play the bad guy more often," he said, leaning up to flick his tongue against my earlobe. "It turns me on."

I chuckled, capturing his lips once more. "I guess it's true what they say, then. Maybe the bad guys do have more fun."

"Oh, they definitely do," he purred. "Come here, and I'll show you."

The End.